The Friendly Little War of Lyman Cutler

Michael Bunnell

Skookum Bay Publishing

Skookum Bay Publishing
copyright©2015 by Michael Bunnell

All rights reserved. No part of this book may be used or reproduced in any manner without written permission except for brief quotations in reviews and critical articles.

ISBN 978-0-9905949-0-1

Cover Illustration by Priscilla Patterson

*To Judi,
who is the reason for everything I do*

Introduction

This book is what's called a *novelization:* a screenplay (movie script) fleshed out into sentences and paragraphs to create a work of prose fiction. Whereas a *treatment* (or *outline,* as Hollywood often calls it) is a much shorter prose *description* of the story, a novelization actually *tells* the story.

Since a novelization is often written by someone other than the original screenwriter, and since the original screenplay may have been revised by anyone from the producer's companion to the director's Jaguar mechanic, novelizations are esteemed by literary critics about as highly as a mongrel is by the judges at an AKC dog show. On the other hand, they're read and enjoyed by a large cross-section of the population which includes many of the more serious literary types: you and I, for example, represent that cross-over element.

The more serious type of novel is almost always experimental in one way or another. Joyce tried that stream-of-consciousness thing in *Ulysses* and managed to pull it off fairly well. Tolkein didn't do too badly with Middle-earth and its inhabitants in *The Hobbit* and *The Lord of the Rings.* Tolstoy wandered so far off into philosophical discourse in *War and Peace* that he claimed it wasn't really a novel at all, but literary experts continue to put it at or near the top of their lists of great novels.

Without presuming to place myself alongside those writers, it's perhaps worth noting one thing we all have in common: each of us is the originator and sole creator of his finished work.

I lived for two years on the site of the events that frame this story. I did the research necessary to write a historically accurate novel, and I wrote the first few chapters. Over the years, I revised and added to the manuscript but never finished it. Then I wrote a screenplay based on the material I'd collected. And then I withdrew the submission when the studio insisted on imposing unacceptable conditions on the project.

Now I've converted the script into this novelization. And in a nod to literary tradition, I've used it as grounds for an experiment: I've tried to combine some elements of a screenplay, a treatment, and a pitch meeting (where the screenwriter "pitches" or tries to sell the project) with the conventions of prose fiction. We'll see how that works out.

The central conflict of my story and the most preposterous incidents are historically correct. With few exceptions, the real people portrayed here really said and did most of the things I have them saying and doing, although in a few cases I've had them speak words which they actually wrote. When I've enlarged upon their words or invented supporting actions, those words and actions are compatible with historical fact and, in most cases, with the natures and objectives of the characters. The only significant exception is my fictionalized portrayal of Charles Griffin, which does nothing to alter the historical accuracy of the plot.

Of course, the purely fictional characters I've created can say and do whatever I want them to; but whenever their roles include things actually done by real people, those actions are faithful to what really happened.

It has distressed me more than you might imagine to take some liberties with a few details: the layout of a town, the location of a moorage, the passage of time, the relative signficance of certain characters. My conscience is soothed only by my intention to follow this book with a scrupulously accurate account of what took place in the San Juan Islands on the eve of the Civil War.

To my fellow sticklers for accuracy I apologize for such liberties as those just noted and also for simplifying some procedures and for using layman's terms for some specialized items. A little technical talk (*taffrail* or *amidships*, for example) or slang from the historical period (*hooch*, for example) here and there may add interest; but as a general rule I'd rather give a few experts something to criticize than confuse the masses of non-experts who will, no doubt, be reading this modest volume.

But enough of that. Let us now adjourn to a small island in a far corner of the United States and the spring of 1859.

The fog that comes to the Strait of Juan de Fuca can be, in some ways, a thing of mystery. It may slide in slowly from the Pacific Ocean in a seemingly impenetrable gray wall that gradually engulfs the lower end of Vancouver Island and the San Juan Islands to the north, the Olympic Peninsula shoreline to the south, and the eighteen-mile-wide span of water between them. This wall of fog typically blends into a sky of the same color so that nothing else is visible above or beyond it.

At other times the fog may drift up from the southeast out of Admiralty Inlet, which is the gateway to Puget Sound, or down from the north out of Rosario Strait, Georgia Strait, or Haro Strait. In these cases, the blue sky over your head extends away from you above the billowing, sometimes wispy top edge of the oncoming wall and highlights the mountain peaks in the background until you and the wall merge and the sky is gone.

On a day of high overcast, however, the gray ceiling may seem to settle gradually toward the ground or the water until, having ignored it for a while, you happen to look around and discover that you're in the process of becoming fogged in. On such a day, the distinctions between fog and low clouds become irrelevant.

The fog may first manifest itself as wisps and thin veils at ground or water level which, somehow without you noticing, rise and expand to fill your world.

Usually, though, you won't notice how the fog arrives, because it usually arrives during the night. You wake up in the morning, and the boundaries of your world are the nearest branches of trees that, on the opposite side, fade away into the fog; or, if you're aboard a ship, you may look either fore or aft and see the railings of your vessel apparently fading away. If you stand at the rail peering into the fog and then look down, the surface of the water appears to extend a few feet further away from the vessel than you can see when you look directly into the wall of mist, producing the odd illusion that the entire fog bank is riding a few feet above the surface.

If you're in a rowboat, you may not be able to see much further into the fog than the tips of your oars. This can be disconcerting when the smiling face of a seal suddenly appears on the water's surface or when you hear the gentle lapping of ripples against something solid and the prolonged *whoosh* which, accompanied by the smell of partially digested fish, tells you that a whale has surfaced just beyond your range of sight and exhaled mightily through the blow hole at the top of its head.

No matter how the fog arrives and how long it stays, you're not likely to notice when it starts to dissipate. At some point, you'll glance up and see that the haze is brighter overhead than at ground or water level, verifying that the sun is up there shining away per its job description. Shortly thereafter, another upward glance will show that the overhead veil is getting thinner. Not too long after that, you'll be surprised to see clear blue sky overhead even though the ground or water is still well shrouded. You'll go on with whatever you're doing, and the next time you look around you'll discover that another fog-free day is in progress.

On just such a foggy morning in 1859, four British marines named Alf, Tom, Will, and Jack crouched behind rocks and scattered evergreen trees on an otherwise uncluttered hillside. Periodically, one of them would creep, hunched but alert, across an expanse of ground cover consisting of a sod-like substance resembling compressed peat moss sprinkled with delicate flowering plants that stood at most two inches high. Occasional tufts of buff-colored calf-high grass lent very little variety to the ground.

The pay-off at the end of the marines' hunched creeping was the shelter of another rock, another tree trunk, or a bush. A less immediate pay-off was the fact that they were gradually if unsystematically working their way uphill into thinner fog which provided better visibility.

Behind his own rock, a young American civilian named Lyman Cutler crouched with his Kentucky rifle at the ready while he listened to every rustle and thump nearby, every footstep, every swish or slap of a low-hanging tree branch momentarily displaced. His face, while not precisely handsome, had been assembled with a set of regular features and a pair of eyes that, when not focused intently on an urgent task, could twinkle with infectious good humor. His well-muscled frame was of a height and proportion to inspire confidence among his friends and caution among others. At the moment, his eyes were focused intently on the task at hand.

A gunshot rang out, much too close to be muffled by the fog. Cutler rose slightly, rested his rifle barrel across the top of his rock, and fired. Another gunshot rang out as he ran crouching to the shelter of a tree trunk, where he quickly reloaded.

"Damn," Alf swore under his breath. "Missed the bugger."

At a sound of movement in front of him, Cutler bolted into the open. He had run only a few steps before another gunshot rang out and he staggered and fell to the ground. Jack darted out of the fog, knelt beside him with his rifle poised, and fired into the fog in the direction Cutler had been running.

Jack was fumbling to reload his rifle when the sounds

of rustling and thumping came from a patch of bushes ahead. Cutler thrust his own rifle at Jack, whispering, "It's loaded."

Jack took Cutler's rifle, crept forward, knelt and fired, then hurried ahead into an opening in the bushes.

Cutler, using Jack's rifle for support, got to his feet and hobbled uphill into a patch of sunshine where he found a rock suitable for sitting and eased himself down onto it. Alf, Tom, Will, and Jack soon joined him, each clutching a rifle in one hand and the hind legs of several dead rabbits in the other.

There will be no better moment than this to mention that all four marines were in the same mid-to-late-twenties age group as Cutler; that Alf was just above the minimum height for Her Majesty's service but was agile, quick-witted, and impetuous; that Tom was about Cutler's height but slender and, though good-natured, was less jovial than some of his associates; that Will was of medium height and exceptionally competent at whatever he was assigned to do, which made his moments of levity all the more engaging for their element of surprise; and that Jack was the only one of the four who ever seriously considered making a career of military service.

As Jack and Cutler exchanged rifles, Jack asked, "You all right, Lyman?"

"Yep. I'm okay."

"What's going on?" asked Tom.

Cutler grinned and said, "I stepped in a rabbit hole." He rubbed his ankle and winced. "Nothing broken, though."

"Well, that's one for the rabbits anyway," said Will.

Jack said, "I swear, Lyman, I've never seen the man that could shoot like you. Don't you ever miss?"

"Seems a shame to go to the trouble of loading her and aiming her and pulling the trigger and not get something to show for it."

Will and Alf grinned at this homespun philosophy of marksmanship as they laid out the dead rabbits.

"How'd we do?" Cutler asked.

"Fourteen," Will reported. "Six of 'em are yours."

As the marines sat on low rocks or on the ground, Cutler said, "Nope. They're all yours. If your cook's gonna make up a mess of hossen-whatever-it-is for your whole outfit, he'll need 'em all."

The five men gazed out across a sea of fog with a few tree-topped islands protruding into the sunlight and, in every direction except due west, rugged snow-capped mountain ranges in the background floating improbably on the fluffy surface.

"Hard to believe there's water under there," said Cutler.

"You've got to know where to look," said Alf, pointing to a patch of water a mile away that showed through the mist between two islands.

Will pointed toward a larger patch where the fog had cleared enough for the sunlight to sparkle on the water.

"That's Haro Strait," he said. "Victoria's directly behind that spot. But a few miles farther away."

Tom pointed to the base of their hill where the fog had thinned enough to reveal small patches of water through the ubiquitous evergreen boughs and the peeling red bark of madrona trunks and branches.

"And it's hard to believe there's a landing beach down there," said Cutler.

Tom smiled and said, "You'd be lucky to spot it on the clearest day God ever created. Can't see it from land for the trees, and too small to be noticed from the water. That's why we use it."

"That brings me back to something I've been wondering about," Cutler said. "Why aren't you supposed to be here?"

"Because," explained Will, "the boundary negotiators agreed not to land any military forces on these islands until they can figure out who owns them."

Cutler, laughing, said, "No offense intended, boys, but I don't think the U. S. Army'd be too worried about four off-duty marines doing a little rabbit hunting."

Jack scowled and replied, "Maybe not. But if it was four Yankee soldiers, you can bet Governor Douglas wouldn't stand for it."

"Besides," Will added, "we're not exactly off duty. More like shirking our duty."

Tom, saying, "Well, I don't want to start a war", stood,

retrieved his rifle, and bent to pick up some rabbits. The other marines did the same.

Alf held his rabbits out toward Cutler, saying, "You sure?"

Cutler waved them away and said, "You can buy me a drink next time we're all over at Whatcom. For me, that'll be later today."

Jack said, "For us, I don't know. We're supposed to meet the *Beaver* up at the north end in about an hour, but I don't know where she's headed after that."

Cutler watched his friends walk down through the vanishing fog and into the trees. A moment later they appeared on a tiny gravel beach, dragging a four-oared gig down to the water's edge. They shoved the boat most of the way into the water; then Tom and Jack steadied it as Alf and Will climbed in at the bow and stepped aft. Then Tom and Jack shoved it further out, vaulting aboard just as the boat floated free.

Lingering on the hilltop, Cutler looked westward again toward Victoria. The bulk of Vancouver Island now loomed dimly in the mist. To the north, what had appeared as two tiny islands a quarter of an hour earlier were now revealed as high points of the island he was standing on. Patches of thin fog remained in the valleys that connected them.

He turned and crossed to the opposite side of the hill, at first favoring his injured ankle, then testing its limits as he reached a downhill path winding among patches of bushes and through clumps of trees.

Cutler's path emerged from the trees on fairly level ground which, to the right, followed the curve of a low bluff overlooking a bay. That area was mostly open; but back near the trees it gave way to patches of salal, blackberry, and wild rose bushes. To the left was the corner of a picket fence which surrounded a farmhouse with a spacious yard in front and along both sides; this yard was not planted with a lawn and ornamental flowers, but the ground cover and bushes inside the fence showed evidence of regular grooming. Behind the house, the fence extended to enclose an area that appeared to be a vegetable garden with a large cedar tree in one corner. Beyond the garden were a large barn, a row of cabins, and grassland leading up to another stand of evergreen trees.

Above the gate in the fence hung a professionally lettered sign reading *Bellevue Farm.*

The path bordered the fence and then curved downhill until it merged with another path, wider and more heavily traveled, which descended to the expanse of low ground at the water's edge.

Cutler paused at the gate, cast an appreciative glance at the farm, and then looked out over the bay. A pier, unusually long and solidly constructed for such a rustic setting, jutted well out into the water. Two steamships were tied up at the pier. Both were less than half the length of a typical ocean-going steamer but larger than most of the vessels that might have been expected to call at such a remote location.

From the foot of the pier, a gravel beach curved along the base of the bluff. In the other direction, the low ground rose to a wooded headland.

Near where the two paths converged was a small wooden structure that might have been either a dwelling or a workshop. It had a door, a window, and a stovepipe in the places where a homesteader's cabin would logically have those features; but much of the structure, though fully roofed and walled on three sides, was completely open on the fourth side. In point of fact, this was both the home and the principal work place of Jeremiah Long, whose career consisted of, as he put it, making and fixing things.

A little distance away, in the shelter of the bluff, was a log cabin and, beside it, a tall, narrow structure something like a pump house with smoke drifting up from a primitive chimney. This was the domain of Cyrus Wilson, who earned his living by smoking things: venison, rabbit, fish, ham, beef, turkey, and specialty items on request.

Several other cabins or huts near the beach provided seasonal lodging for fishermen.

Two long rowboats, each with an elevated platform at one end, were pulled up onto the beach. Between the boats and a tent near the bluff, above the high-tide line, two men were spreading a fishing net out to dry.

Cutler's attention was diverted from his survey of this scene by shouts from the direction of the Bellevue Farm barn.

Near the barn, one man directed the movements of

three others who darted back and forth helping a collie drive a dozen or more sheep through an opening in a primitive fence and back into their pen. One of the farmhands tripped over the fallen section of fence that had allowed the sheep to escape.

Cutler smiled and muttered, "Gotta be an easier way to make a buck" as he continued down the path to the water.

One of the vessels at the pier was the *Sylvia*, flying the American flag. She was a screw-driven steamer with an enclosed lower deck that made it look as if the upper deck and the wheelhouse were perched atop a boat-shaped barn. A few farm wives clustered around the Purser as he stepped onto the pier through the open cargo door of the lower deck. He handed out letters from a leather pouch, then collected outgoing mail from the farm wives, climbed back aboard the *Sylvia*, and stuffed the outgoing mail into a large canvas sack beside the doorway.

The steamer on the other side of the pier was the sidewheeler *Beaver*, flying the English Union Jack. Since her paddle wheels, one on each side mounted near the forward end of the vessel, left a sizeble gap between the pier and the ship's deck, a gangplank had been run out. A crewman with a leather pouch slung over one shoulder crossed the gangplank and stood on the pier, handing letters to two farm wives who then joined those turning away from the *Sylvia*. The women all left the pier together in friendly conversation.

Cutler nodded and smiled at the women as he stepped onto the pier. As he hurried toward the *Sylvia*, where two deckhands were making ready to cast off her lines, he called, "Whatcom?"

"Three stops to make first," replied the nearest deckhand. "Oughta be there around two o'clock."

Cutler stepped aboard through the cargo door. The deckhands tossed their coiled ropes through the door, then leaned hard against the *Sylvia* until she started to move away from the pier. Then they jumped aboard.

Charles Griffin, the manager of Bellevue Farm, and Joe, a farmhand, came onto the pier as the *Sylvia* drifted far enough away to begin slowly swinging around. Griffin had been the supervisor of the sheepherding operation that had amused Cutler, and Joe had been the farmhand who had tripped over the fallen section of fence.

Griffin was an amiable-looking man who might have been in his late forties or early fifties. He stood and moved as a man does who is accustomed to physical labor and prepared, if not over-eager, to do more of it. He also gave the impression of being aware of the social graces but not in the habit of allowing them to interfere with efficiency or comfort. He was, in fact, what the British called a "younger son": not in line to inherit the family's estate, but sufficiently well-off to have a choice of paths in life. He could have entered government or quasi-government service in an administrative capacity, but he had shown an early inclination toward roughing it in out-of-the-way corners of the British Empire. It was this inclination that had brought him to San Juan Island.

The *Beaver's* crewman shrugged the strap off his shoulder, started to hand the pouch to Griffin, then paused uncertainly.

"Joe's here for the mail as usual," Griffin replied, taking the pouch and handing it to Joe.

"No cargo for the farm today," said the crewman.

"Didn't expect any. I'm coming with you."

To Joe, Griffin said, "Have a couple of the men's wives give the house a look-over. The woman's touch, don't you know. And do whatever you can to spruce up the garden."

The Captain of the *Beaver* came to the gangplank and greeted Griffin: "Fetching the mail in person today?"

Griffin said, "Meeting my niece at Whatcom. Her father... my brother, don't you know... has been running one of those spice islands out east... well, west from here... Mary's going home to London a little early... staying with me until her father wraps things up with the local wallahs and so forth."

Griffin crossed the gangplank as the *Beaver's* deckhands prepared to cast off.

Out in the bay, the *Sylvia* had turned and was steaming away around the wooded headland.

Three thousand miles away, President James Buchanan swiveled his chair for a more comfortable view of the easel standing at the end of his desk and tried to look interested in the map of the United States that rested on it. On the other side of the desk, General William Harney stood glaring at the easel, making no effort to feign interest.

Archibald Campbell, a young diplomat, stood beside the easel. At a nod from the President, he picked up a pointer and used it to indicate the northern boundary of the United States.

"As you know, the Treaty of Oregon established the 49th parallel as the boundary between the United States and British territory from the Great Lakes all the way to the western coast."

Campbell traced the boundary with his pointer.

"As you say," growled Harney, "we knew that."

A large fly entered through the open window, lazily circled the easel, and started to settle on Campbell's pointer. Campbell twitched the pointer to dislodge the fly and almost dropped the pointer.

"The treaty further established that when the boundary reached the water separating Vancouver Island from the mainland, it would follow the middle of the channel to the Strait of Juan de Fuca."

He traced an imaginary line around the tip of Vancouver Island which extended south of the 49th parallel.

"From there it would follow the middle of the strait until it met the ocean." The pointer led all eyes out to sea.

The fly circled in front of Campbell's face. He swatted

ineffectually. It landed on the easel. Campbell fluttered a hand and the fly abandoned its position. Campbell placed a second map on the easel.

"This, I believe, will indicate…" was as far as he got before the fly landed on his map. Campbell flicked a finger in the fly's direction, dropped his pointer on the floor, bumped his head on the desk as he stooped to retrieve it, and did a barely adequate job of regaining his composure as he stood up again.

Harney snatched a newspaper off the President's desk, folded it, and lashed out, scattering the easel, the maps, and the now-deceased fly across the floor.

Tossing the newspaper back onto the desk, he demanded, "Now will you tell us what the hell your problem is?"

Campbell hastily re-erected his easel, scooped up his maps, scouted around and found his pointer, then replaced the second map on the easel. It was identical to the first map except for a dozen small islands and scores of dots in the water separating Vancouver Island from the mainland.

Campbell moved the tip of his pointer slowly around these islands and dots.

Buchanan leaned forward, genuinely interested at last.

"These are the San Juan Islands," explained Campbell. "There may be a hundred or more, counting every rock that shows above high tide. At least a dozen are of significant size."

"And are they important?" Buchanan asked.

Campbell, warming to his subject, continued with spirit: "They contain many fine bays and harbors. San Juan Island itself lies along the Strait of Juan de Fuca, where shore batteries on the high ground could protect access to Puget Sound. It has at least two deep harbors that could accommodate a merchant fleet as well as naval vessels."

Campbell placed a third map on the easel. It was a close-up of the southern tip of Vancouver Island, the San Juan Islands, the Strait of Juan de Fuca, the continental shoreline, and Puget Sound.

"Whoever controls San Juan Island," he went on, "controls access to the most extensive system of deep-water harbors, overland transportation routes, and natural resources in the world."

President Buchanan looked impressed. General Harney looked impatient.

"You still haven't told us what the problem is," Harney said.

Campbell met Harney's glare for a moment, then quickly looked at Buchanan.

"The problem is that these islands aren't shown on the maps that were used to negotiate the Treaty of Oregon. They're not mentioned in the treaty. So it's not clear whether they're American or British."

Harney laughed contemptuously.

"There's the power of diplomacy for you."

Campbell went on: "Our position is that the treaty

meant only to divert the boundary line far enough to include all of Vancouver Island within British territory. But Governor Douglas claims them as part of British Columbia, and he's adamant in his position. He has made no secret of his anger at the negotiators who ceded the Columbia River and Puget Sound to the United States, and he's inflexible on the issue of these islands."

Buchanan asked, "Who's in possession of them at this moment?"

"Most of the islands are uninhabited," said Campbell. "There are some English and American settlers on San Juan Island. And the Hudson's Bay Company has a sheep farm there."

"Troops!" shouted Harney. "How many troops do we have, and how many do they have?"

Campbell, still looking at Buchanan, replied, "Both sides have agreed not to place military forces on the islands until the boundary issue is resolved."

"If Americans live there, it's American territory," declared Harney. "And if it's American territory, I'll defend it!"

Buchanan, more resigned than irritated, asked, "Defend it against what, General?"

"Why, against foreign aggression and…"

"Let me remind you, General, that you have not yet taken command out there. When you do assume your duties, you are not to take any action that will threaten or antagonize our neighbors."

"And if a foreign power violates American sovereignty or the rights of our citizens? Do I just stand around" (glancing at Campbell) "like a scared schoolboy?"

"Certainly you'll be expected to maintain our sovereignty and our national honor," the President replied.

"That's all I wanted to know."

Harney turned and started to walk away.

"General Harney."

Harney paused and looked back at Buchanan.

"Just remember that this is a diplomatic problem, not a military one. We're not at war."

"But we'll be ready if it comes. Sir." And Harney left the office.

Campbell returned his maps to their case and folded his easel but remained standing beside Buchanan's desk.

"Was there anything else, Mister Campbell?"

"Well. As a matter of fact…yes, Mister President. As head of our delegation to the boundary negotiations, I can't help worrying about General Harney's approach…his… well, I mean, he has a record of being…"

"Hot-headed? Undisciplined? Self-serving?"

Campbell nodded and said, "His grounds for hanging those Indians in Florida seemed…perhaps…somewhat flimsy. And his effort to hang Brigham Young in Utah showed, if I may say so, perhaps more vigor and less tact than the situation called for."

Buchanan leaned back and replied, "You're absolutely right."

Campbell added, "It's been said that General Scott recently removed General Harney from his command but that he refused to step down...and that General Scott was over-ruled by General Harney's political cronies."

Buchanan pushed his chair away from the desk, stood slowly, paced to the window, and came back to stand behind his chair.

"It's true. General Harney has more political influence than the Commanding General of the United States Army has. Probably more than I have."

Placing both hands on the back of his chair, Buchanan went on: "He'd like to be sitting here, and quite frankly he's welcome to. Secession may not come during my term, but the next man who sits here will surely have it to contend with."

"I wonder, Mister President...as a Southerner, General Harney might find it expedient to embroil the country in some manner of conflict before the Southern states left the Union. It would spare the separatist states from receiving our full military attention. And a foreign conflict could give them an ally against us."

"He's being sent out to the most remote and peaceful spot on this continent precisely to limit his opportunities for stirring up trouble," Buchanan replied. "You've been there, Mister Campbell. What do you think?"

"Well...the American and English settlers appear to get along well. Trouble with the Indians is infrequent. The prospectors bound for the Fraser River generally head north from one of our ports and ignore Governor Douglas's demand that they register with British authorities in Victoria, but he hasn't ordered any action against them."

"And the American authorities?"

"I'm acquainted with Colonel Casey, who commands our forces in the Puget Sound country. He seems quite level-headed, and he supports our diplomatic mission. I've met Captain Pickett, who commands an infantry company at Fort Bellingham a few miles from the border: an intelligent and well-spoken gentleman, but…like General Harney, a Southerner."

Buchanan smiled and replied, "The goat of his West Point class. Lowest marks in the class of Forty-six. Captain Pickett isn't likely to leave his name in the annals of our nation's history."

"May I point out, though," said Campbell, "that he was the first man to scale the ramparts at Chapultapec in the Mexican War and that he has the classic Southerner's contempt for danger? And the classic Southerner's obsession with honor? And that his colonel, and by extension he himself, will take orders from General Harney?"

"Don't you worry about that. Just go back out there and wrap up the diplomatic problem. I don't think Captain Pickett or General Harney will be in a position to cause us any trouble."

The hustle and bustle, ebb and flow, coming and going, loading and unloading that characterized the waterfront community of Whatcom might have led an observer with a modestly creative imagination to compare it with a bee hive or an ant hill.

A more prosaic observer would have noted the ocean-going steamships and sailing ships which were moored at the long pier and the others which were anchored out in Bellingham Bay. Such an observer would also have noted that the pier and anchorage were shared by smaller ships that carried passengers, freight, and mail from Whatcom through the San Juan Islands and along the coast of the "inland waters" to Puget Sound.

A major contributor to the waterfront activity was the lumber mill which sent a steady flow of ships to San Francisco with materials that were in high demand as that city continued to rebuild after its disastrous fire.

Another major contributor was the rush for gold in the Fraser River Valley just north of the border, which was only a few miles away. This drew thousands of inbound passengers who were either ignorant or contemptuous of Governor James Douglas's decree that anyone crossing the border must register with the British authorities in Victoria, which was fifty miles away to the west across at least three bodies of water and accessible only by sailing around the San Juan Islands or through their maze of passages and channels.

Along the miles of beaches around the bay, but especially at those near the pier, every type of small craft from canoes to sailboats could be seen pulled up on the sand or gravel. Those too big to be pulled entirely out of the water, or those that had been left floating at high tide and were still, as the tide went out, more or less afloat, were secured by long ropes tied around driftwood logs on the beach or to small trees just beyond the driftwood.

In the background, so to speak, was the shipping activity connected with the coal mine at Sehome, a separate shoreline village.

Also in the background was Fort Bellingham, situated on a bluff with a fine view of the bay.

A chandlery, a general store, a hardware store, a blacksmith's shop, a gunsmith's shop, a barbershop, two pawn shops, three hotels, four cafes, and seven saloons were within a few blocks of the Whatcom waterfront.

Ships newly arrived from San Francisco and Seattle

disgorged a flow of prospectors and settlers eager to get ashore and fulfill their hopes for a new life. Loungers and drifters just as eagerly and hopefully alternated between panhandling and trying to waylay a ship's officer in an effort to wangle free passage on an outbound vessel. Longshoremen with hand trucks and teamsters with freight wagons added further interest to the scene.

Norbert Higgins, a man in his early to mid thirties who would be described by almost anyone who encountered him as "average" in every respect, walked onto the pier. He was accompanied… some might have said *supervised*… by Minverva, his wife, a woman of comparably average size but with a commanding presence that kept any inclination toward assertiveness on her husband's part well under control.

After walking a few yards along the pier, Higgins stopped to look things over; but his wife, for reasons best known to herself, nudged him toward the *Beaver*, saying, "That must be our boat."

When her husband continued to stand and observe, she said. "Well, go on. Tell the Captain you're ready to have your merchandise loaded."

"But, my dear, I'm not. The wagon isn't here yet."

"Well, *you're* here. You can at least tell them to be ready."

She nudged him more forcefully toward the *Beaver*. Higgins took a few steps, then stopped and said, "My dear, I don't…"

"I should think you could at least go and introduce yourself", she said.

"But, my dear, I think this is the wrong boat. Or ship. You see, it's flying the English flag. I think that one is ours."

Higgins pointed to the *Sylvia*, which was tied up just beyond the *Beaver*.

"Well, then, what are you standing *here* for?" she demanded, nudging him toward the *Sylvia*.

Cutler and a few other passengers stepped off the *Sylvia*. Higgins stood aside as they passed; then he approached the Purser standing on the pier examining a paper and said, "Good afternoon. Is this the boat that goes to San Juan Island?"

"We've been there once today," said the Purser, "but we're scheduled to stop there again with a freight shipment on our way back down to the sound." He glanced at his paper. "Are you Norbert Higgins?"

"Yes, sir. Hardware and dry goods. I expect my merchandise to arrive at any moment. I'll just go and see…"

Higgins hurried back the way he had come.

Sam Pike and Ike Webster hailed Cutler as he approached the foot of the pier. Pike was a weathered veteran of two gold rushes who probably wasn't as much older than Cutler as he looked and, if he had cared more about how he dressed, might have been considered better looking. Webster was a little younger than Pike, a little taller than Cutler, and no more ambitious than either of them. As

Cutler joined his friends, three men with knapsacks, picks, and shovels passed them heading ashore.

Pike called out, "Forget it, gents."

"Forget what?" answered one of the prospectors. "We're heading north."

"It's a bust," Pike said.

"But the San Francisco papers are full of the Fraser River Gold Rush."

"Fraser River Humbug is more like it," Webster said. "Ain't enough gold up there to fill a tooth."

He made a sweeping gesture that took in twenty or thirty loungers and drifters.

"Just ask any of these fellas," he said.

One of the other prospectors said, "Well, I think we'll just go find out for ourselves."

As the prospectors trudged uphill into the town, a detachment of U. S. soldiers marched down to the pier led by Captain George Pickett on horseback. The soldiers were followed by a mule-drawn wagon filled with bushel baskets of vegetables.

Miss La Belle, an entrepreneur of sorts, and Nicole, Martine, and Giselle, three of her associates, strolled past the pier and caught Pickett's eye.

Miss La Belle greeted him with, "Captain Pickett, you do look dashing today. As always, of course."

Pickett, touching the brim of his hat with his riding crop, replied, "Miss La Belle. Ladies. May I say that you're looking quite… Parisian?"

"Why, thank you, Captain. And may I inquire how your garden is coming along?"

"It prospers, thank you," Pickett replied.

Gesturing toward the wagon, he added, "As you see, we're sending produce to the forts down on Puget Sound."

Miss La Belle asked, "Why don't the forts down on the sound grow their own produce?"

"I believe they make an effort; but we apparently have more favorable weather conditions here," said Pickett. "Less rain and fog."

At a command from their sergeant, the soldiers broke formation: three of them went out onto the pier while the others began unloading the wagon.

Miss La Belle and her girls continued on their way, the girls exchanging winks and smiles with the soldiers in passing.

Mary Griffin, a young English aristocrat, and Marlene Potts, her maid, walked from the biggest hotel down to the pier followed by Alf, Tom, and Will carrying their luggage.

Mary had the delicate features and the pampered complexion which, along with a careful upbringing that placed major emphasis on charm and grace, made her more attractive than nature might have intended her to be. Auburn hair meticulously coiffed and a wardrobe selected with no consideration of expense contributed to that air of haughty vulnerability which Victorian men, always suckers for a good paradox, found so alluring.

Her maid had a simpler and more direct appeal. Of grace and charm she had her fair share, as befitted the attendant of a young lady of the privileged class. But her shapely form was not entirely disguised by the attire that came with her station in life, and the black hair that often defied convention by tumbling down around her cheeks drew attention to a pair of large blue eyes that, on their own, were fully capable of ensnaring any man's heart.

As the marines passed the American soldiers, Alf grinned and said, "Taken up farming, have you?"

Sutherland, one of the soldiers, responded: "Had to, seein' as Her Majesty's marines have cornered the baggage-carryin' trade."

Tom said, "All in a day's work, mate. We do what we're told."

"Ain't that the truth," agreed Sutherland.

McCleary, another soldier, said to the passing marines as he stacked bushel baskets handed down to him from the wagon, "Hurry back and we'll have some more for you to carry."

Will, supporting a trunk on his shoulder with one hand, used his free hand to salute McCleary with a crisp, "Aye, aye, sir!"

McCleary and Will grinned at each other.

Gorst, another soldier, nodded toward Mary and her maid and said to Will, "For two cents I'll trade places with you."

On the pier, Charles Griffin was waiting for his niece.

"Mary?" he asked in surprise. "I mean, er, have I the honor of addressing Miss Griffin?"

Mary laughed.

"Yes, Uncle Charles. So you didn't recognize me?"

"Well, my dear girl, you were so much younger the last time I saw you. Pigtails, don't you know, and a short frock."

Griffin glanced from Mary to Marlene and back, politely but uncertainly.

"This is Potts. My maid."

Griffin bowed slightly, murmuring, "A pleasure, Miss Potts." To Mary: "Might as well get aboard ship, I suppose."

He turned and found the way partially blocked by Cutler and his friends. When he hesitated, Marlene stepped ahead of him calling, "Excuse us, gents. Lady and a gentleman coming through *if* you please!"

Cutler, Pike, and Webster stepped back to let them pass. Cutler smiled at Marlene, whose face remained impassive until Mary looked away; then she returned the smile. Mary looked their way again in time to see Cutler wink.

"Uncle Charles," Mary whispered, "that fellow just… looked very impertinently at Potts."

Griffin, glancing at Cutler and seeing only a polite smile on his face, said, "Well, you know, we're a bit informal out here. Good people on the frontier, you know, but possibly not quite the style you've been used to."

Marlene waited for Mary and her uncle to precede her

again, holding a dignified pose until they had passed; then she glanced back, winked at Cutler, and hurried on to rejoin her employer.

Alf, Will, and Tom lingered to exchange greetings with Cutler.

"Where's Jack?" Cutler asked.

Tom answered as one conspirator to another: "He had a delivery to make to the company cook."

"Glad that worked out," Cutler said. Nodding toward Pike and Webster, he went on: "These are the fellas that helped me strike it rich up on the Fraser. Ike, Sam, these pack mules are Alf, Tom, and Will."

Alf said, "Struck it rich, eh?"

Webster answered, "You bet. But we can't decide whether to spend our fortune on a beer or a haircut."

As the marines moved on toward the *Beaver*, a freight wagon clattered onto the pier. The teamster hauled back on the reins, set the brake, and shouted, "Dry goods for Higgins!"

"That's me!" called Higgins, pushing as politely as possible through the two-way flow of humanity on the pier which now included longshoremen wheeling hand trucks of vegetable baskets to the *Sylvia*.

The three soldiers who had gone out onto the pier came back with their arms full of garden implements, some of which they dropped as they stepped aside to let Mary and Marlene pass. A member of the cadging-free-drinks profession, clearly having enjoyed a successful day, collided with a pitchfork as it fell, clutched it, staggered backward, then came to an unsteady version of attention with the pitchfork at shoulder arms. Other loungers laughed and cheered; one of them stood at attention and saluted.

Thus encouraged, the one with the pitchfork shouted, "Hup, two, three, four" and marched two steps before staggering and pointing the pitchfork like a rifle. Mary backed quickly away from him, bumped one of the horses hitched to the wagon, lost her balance and fell.

The well-oiled gentleman whirled, staggered, brandished the pitchfork as if to fend off the stamping horses. The horses reared up. Mary was about to be trampled.

Cutler shoved the man aside, dragged Mary to safety, then stepped between the horses and grabbed their halters, calming them down.

Marlene and Griffin rushed to Mary and knelt beside her. Cutler released the horses, stepped over to Mary, leaned down and extended his hand. She hesitated, then took his hand and allowed him to help her up. She fell against him, breathing heavily; but the moment she regained her balance she hastily backed away.

"Are you all right, my dear?" asked her uncle.

"Yes. Thanks to this…" She looked uncertainly at Cutler.

Marlene leaned toward her and whispered, "This impertinent fellow?"

Griffin grabbed Cutler's hand, shaking it vigorously, saying, "By gad, sir, that was well done!"

"My pleasure," Cutler replied.

"Charles Griffin, sir. My niece, Mary…" (Griffin belatedly remembered the demands of formality) "that is to say, Miss Griffin."

"How do you do, Miss Griffin? I'm Lyman Cutler." Turning to Marlene: "And this young lady?"

"Potts," Mary replied. "My maid."

"A pleasure to meet you, Miss Potts."

"Thank you, sir," said Marlene demurely.

"No need to call me *sir*. You could call me…"

"I believe our ship is waiting," Mary said.

"Where are you bound for?" Cutler asked. "That is, if you don't mind me asking."

Griffin said, "San Juan Island."

"No kidding," said Cutler. "What do you do out there?"

"Oh, run some sheep, don't you know, and that sort of thing."

"My uncle," said Mary austerely, "is too modest. He is the manager of Bellevue Farm."

"Say, I think I saw you out there this morning," Cutler said to Griffin. "Running some sheep, in fact."

Griffin chuckled and replied, "Seemed more like they were running us, don't you think?"

The bell of the *Beaver* clanged.

"That's our boat," said Griffin. To Mary: "Go right

ahead. They're expecting you." To Cutler: "Thank you again, young man, for your…well, dash it, your spendidly courageous action."

"Oh, it was nothing."

Marlene said, "It was the bravest thing I've ever seen," and then hurried away before either man could reply.

Cutler rejoined Pike and Webster, asking, "Well, have you fellas figured out what you're gonna do next?"

Pike said, "I'm for going across to Vancouver Island. They say Victoria's a real boom town."

"Maybe," said Webster. "But it's an English town."

"They say there's ten Americans for every Englishman over there," Pike replied. "And anyway, my pa came from England. I don't guess being English or American would matter very much."

Webster countered with, "I say we head down to Puget Sound. Chances are better there than here for scarin' up enough money to buy passage down to Frisco."

They both looked at Cutler, who was watching the *Beaver*'s deckhands cast off her mooring lines.

"You fellas do whatever you please," he said. "I think I'll go back out to San Juan Island and see what turns up."

The *Sylvia's* whistle screamed as Cutler left his companions and started back along the pier.

A new cabin, apparently built mostly with second-hand lumber and apparently with expediency as a higher priority than workmanship, sat at the edge of a roughly spaded quarter of an acre bounded by wild rose bushes and blackberry vines. The property was most of the way up one side of the hill where Cutler had helped hunt rabbits a week earlier. Here there were no protruding lumps of bedrock offering convenient places to sit or to crouch behind while sneaking up on the ever-present rabbits. There were, however, a few scattered evergreen trees, and the cabin had been built near one of them.

A wheelbarrow stood in the dug-up field. It contained several bulging gunny sacks, a spade, and Cutler's Kentucky rifle.

Cutler dragged a half-full gunny sack along a row of cultivated ground mounded up into hills a few feet apart. He took a seed potato from the sack, sliced it with his hunting knife, sliced each half, planted all four pieces in a hill, then moved on.

Behind Cutler, a very large pig waddled out of a deer path through the bushes and began rooting among the hills Cutler had already planted. At a loud, satisfied snort from the pig, Cutler stood up, whirled around, and shouted "GYAAAAAHHHH!" or something that would have sounded very much like that to a human bystander. To the pig it carried no meaning: without even looking at his interlocutor, the animal continued with its mid-morning snack.

Cutler took a few rapid steps to the wheelbarrow, grabbed his rifle, and took quick aim at the pig. At the same moment, Marlene Potts stepped out of the deer path carrying a basket of wild roses. Seeing the pig, then seeing the barrel of Cutler's rifle pointing at it and her, she screamed and dropped the basket.

"Miss Potts!" Cutler exclaimed, refraining from pulling the trigger. A heartbeat later, he lowered the rifle, returned it to the wheelbarrow, and ran to her. The pig looked up and grunted (perhaps belligerently, since pigs aren't always the docile creatures they often seem to be) as Cutler dodged around it.

Marlene stepped back, alarmed not only by the sound of the pig but also by the intent look in Cutler'e eyes as he sprinted toward her. Something apologetic in his expression made her halt, trembling, as he reached her.

Cutler held her shoulders as she regained her

composure, then stepped back.

"I sure didn't mean to scare you," he said.

"No harm done, sir."

Cutler retrieved the basket and returned it with the somewhat self-evident remark, "Picking flowers, I see."

"Yes, sir. For the dining table. Not but what it seems a shame to take 'em indoors. They don't look so natural there, as you might say."

Cutler said, "I know the perfect place to display wild roses." He took one from the basket and slipped the stem under one of the pins which did their best to hold her unhatted hair in place.

She said, "Oh, sir, I'm sure I don't know if you ought to do that"; but her smile confessed her lack of concern over the propriety of his action.

Cutler asked, "Are you required to call me *sir* just because you're somebody's maid?"

"What would you like me to call you?"

"How about *Lyman*? That's my name."

"Well, I don't know as I could call you that…unless you was to call me *Marlene*."

"*Marlene*," Cutler repeated. "That's a beautiful name. The kind of name songs ought to be written about."

"Potts!" It was Mary's voice coming from somewhere on the other side of the bushes.

Marlene said ruefully, "That part of my name'll never get a song written about it."

"Potts! Where are you?"

Mary came around the end of the patch of bushes as Cutler finished securing the rose in Marlene's hair. Seeing her employer, Marlene quickly stepped back from Cutler.

Mary approached, stepping carefully over the spaded ground, stopping at a safe distance from the pig to say, "Mister Cutler. What are you doing here?"

"Morning, Miss Griffin. I was just, um, helping Marlene...that is, Miss Potts...that is, we..."

"I mean, what are you doing *here*?"

"Oh." Cutler looked around at his cabin and his quarter of an acre of spaded ground. "Farming."

"But you can't farm here," said Mary.

"Oh, it's good soil. Easy to dig. I should get a pretty decent crop of spuds if I can keep that pig out of 'em."

"But you're an American."

"Yep."

"A Yankee."

"We're often called that. But I can't see what that has to do with growing spuds."

"But you're on British territory. The Hudson's Bay Company owns this land. This is one of their sheep runs. My uncle owns this pig."

Charles Griffin and Joe, the farmhand, came around the other end of the row of bushes from the path leading down past the farm to the water. Griffin carried a rustic walking stick. Joe carried a coil of rope with a shackle on one end.

"Here he is, by gad," said Griffin, sharing Cutler's penchant for the obvious.

He strode up to the pig and prodded it with his stick.

"Come away, dash it!" he commanded.

The pig waddled toward the edge of the garden. Joe intercepted it and snapped the shackle of his rope to the ring in the pig's nose.

"Good show, Joe," Griffin said.

As Joe led the pig away, Griffin said, "By gad, that was rather clever, what? Rhymed, you know: *Good show, Joe.*"

He chuckled at his own inadvertent wit and repeated, "*Good show, Joe.* Rather good."

Then, to Cutler, he said, "Glad to see you again, my dear fellow. But what the deuce is all this?"

He waved an arm to indicate Cutler's farming operation.

"It's my potato patch."

"But, my dear fellow, this is one of my sheep runs."

"So I've been informed. Too bad I didn't know that sooner."

Griffin smiled. Cutler grinned. Then they both laughed.

Mary scowled at her uncle, then at Cutler, then glanced at Marlene and caught her smiling. Catching Mary's eye, Marlene immediately scowled, too.

Mary drew herself up haughtily. Behind her back, Marlene resumed her smile.

Mary said, "You'll have to plant your potatoes

somewhere else, Mister Cutler."

"Well," put in Griffin, "hardly that. We can run the sheep on the north slope for another month and then put 'em back on the old run. But, my dear fellow, after you've harvested your crop you really must relocate."

"Sounds fair to me. And for the time being, it looks like we're neighbors."

"Splendid. Well, I suppose I should be getting back. Paperwork to finish before the company boat arrives. Always something, don't you know. But perhaps when you're finished here you'll come down to the house for a spot of something refreshing."

Mary said, "I hardly think Mister Cutler would feel comfortable…"

"I'd be glad to," said Cutler. Then he nodded to Mary and Marlene and returned to his planting.

To Marlene, Mary said: "Potts, you may go on ahead and get those flowers into a bowl of water."

"Yes, Miss," replied Marlene, and she ducked back into the deer path and was gone.

Mary continued to Griffin: "Really, Uncle Charles. Have you no respect for class distinctions?"

"Lot of silly nonsense. All very well for the idle rich, but when you've had to make your own way in the world you learn to respect a man for his own qualities."

"And does Mister Cutler have such very attractive qualities?"

"You mean, besides the fact that he saved your life?"

Mary opened her mouth, then shut it and stalked off with as much dignity as the spaded ground permitted. Griffin shook his head and then followed her down the path.

Colonel Silas Casey sat at his desk in his office at Fort Steilacoom, near Puget Sound in the Washington Territory, which was part of of the region still known colloquially as "the Oregon country". He had just leaned back after finishing an especially tedious round of paperwork and was gazing out the window at the rhodedendron bushes with their dark green leaves looking heavily waxed as they reflected the sunlight. He derived some very unmilitary enjoyment from scrutinizing the hundreds of buds for hints of the red, purple, pink, or white that would burst into bloom within the next few days.

These moments of contentment in a busy life seldom last long, and it was only a moment later when an orderly entered and stood at attention. Casey promptly abandoned his horticultural observation and returned to duty.

"Yes?" he said to the orderly.

"General Harney has arrived, Colonel," the young

man reported.

Pushing back his chair, Casey stood and said, "Show him in."

The orderly turned smartly and bumped into General Harney, who had not waited to be shown in. Stammering a series of attempts at a formal apology, he gave up the effort and hurried from the room.

"Good morning, General," said Casey, motioning toward the chair on Harney's side of the desk.

Harney asked as he sat, "How's the Indian situation out here?"

Casey, in the process of sitting, paused midway through the process in his surprise at the question. Then he sat and said, "I wouldn't say that we have an Indian *situation*, General. The trouble we had over the treaties has calmed down. East of the mountains they're still having some incidents, but over here we have things under control. Now and then our own people cause a stir with some of the locals, but nothing that can't be handled. Once in a while the Haidas come down from British Columbia. They're a warlike bunch, but if they actually attack anybody it's just as likely to be our local Indians."

"They ever kill any white men?"

"Not as often as white men kill them. Most of our dead white men are killed by other white men."

"We may have to get a little tougher in our Indian policy."

"But I've just said they don't often…"

"Now, what about this boundary dispute?"

"It hasn't been a problem. Homesteaders from both sides of the border had settled on San Juan Island before anyone discovered the oversight in the treaty, so of course there's been some rivalry. But our chief negotiator, Mister Campbell, has assured me…"

"Mister Campbell is hardly the man to dictate our military policy. No backbone. Couldn't hurt a fly."

Casey took on a more assertive tone as he said, "General, may I recommend that you take a while to familiarize yourself with…"

"I understand you have an officer named Pickett serving under you."

"Captain Pickett commands an infantry company at Fort Bellingham, just a few miles this side of the border."

"I think I'll have something for him to do in regard to this San Juan Island business."

More formally, Casey said, "May I remind the General that according to military protocol I would be advised of any need for action and would either take that action myself or delegate the responsibility to an officer under my command?"

"Don't lecture me on the chain of command, Colonel Casey."

Harney stood up.

So did Casey.

"I'm in charge of this department," Harney continued, "and I'll give whatever orders I damn well please to any officer I choose."

"I understand, General."

Harney turned his back on Casey and strode out of the office.

Casey, sitting down again, said to himself, "I understand all too well."

~ 5 ~

The path leading down from the center of San Juan Island and through the depression behind the wooded headland near the pier had been cut and trampled into a rough track which bore some resemblance to a road.

The waterfront community now sported a large tent and three tarp-covered stacks of unidentifiable objects. Norbert Higgins stood admiring the sign leaning against one of the stacks: *San Juan Hardware & Dry Goods - Norbert Higgins, Proprietor.*

Creaking, clattering, and the breathing of large animals accompanied by occasional nonverbal exclamations of human origin gave Higgins advance notice that something was about to arrive by way of the "road". Thus he was ready to greet Ian McGregor when his team of draft horses reached the level ground pulling a flatbed wagon loaded with freshly milled lumber.

McGregor, big and strong and unkempt, hauled back on the reins and set the wagon's brake, returned Higgins's greeting with an affable but silent nod, and climbed down.

Minerva Higgins emerged from the tent and stood casting a critical eye at the lumber, the wagon, the horses, McGregor, and from force of habit her husband.

At the sound of a steam whistle, they all looked toward the water and saw the *Beaver* rounding the headland. As it glided silently up to the pier, Griffin came down the path from Bellevue Farm.

"Fine-looking lumber, McGregor," he said.

"Thank you, sir. Though it'd be a hard thing to turn out anything less from the trees on this island."

"Think that little mill of yours could turn out the joists and beams for another big barn?"

"Aye, sir, that it could."

"Come on up to the house when you're through here and I'll show you the plans." To Higgins he said, "Hardware and dry goods, eh? Capital, capital. That's a thing we've needed on this island."

McGregor began loosening the ropes that held the lumber to the wagon.

Zeke, Clarence, and Tubby, American settlers, walked down the road and stopped beside the wagon.

"Right on time, gentlemen," said Higgins cheerfully. "I think we can get it unloaded and get the foundation blocks in place before dinner time."

Sir James Douglas and his aide, Percy Fainworthy, came ashore from the *Beaver* and approached the group at the building site.

Sir James was a stern, robust man who could have been about Griffin's age; but his perpetual look of disapproval and his air of having never done anything frivolous in his life, which must have made him look middle-aged even as a much younger man, were in stark contrast to the qualities that made Griffin appear youthful in spite of his years. Sir James's impeccable grooming and faultless attire did nothing to mitigate the impression that he could, and gladly would, take on any man on any issue either moral, legal, or physical.

Fainworthy was at the age when a man of the upper class has become sophisticated enough to enjoy a fairly wide acquaintance among the ladies but is now expected to select a wife; and he was accustomed to the respect that comes with that status, especially from marriageable young ladies and their mothers. He was also accustomed to the deference typically shown by men whose station in life left them less fashionably attired and not so fastidiously groomed; but unlike Sir James, whose appearance did not diminish his air of command in any group, Fainworthy looked out of place in a frontier setting. Furthermore, he looked like a man who knows he looks out of place.

In some surprise, Griffin said, "Well, Jimmy, what brings you out here?"

Sir James glared at him, and Griffin said, "Oh, sorry. I

mean *Sir James*."

To Higgins and McGregor, Griffin explained: "We started out in the Hudson's Bay Company together, don't you know. Trading blankets to the Indians for otter pelts and all that sort of thing. And now he's the Governor of this colony, and I'm running a sheep farm."

Sir James inquired politely, "How do you do, Charles?"

To Higgins and McGregor, Griffin said, "It used to be *Charley*, but you see we're much more formal now."

"I believe you know my aide, the Honorable Percy Fainworthy."

Fainworthy bowed almost imperceptibly.

Griffin, returning the bow with a similarly noncommittal nod, said, "Yes. My niece and I made his acquaintance the night we stayed over in Victoria."

Fainworthy said, "I was hoping that I might call upon Miss Griffin."

"Call upon her?" said Griffin. "Oh, ah. Yes, of course. Go right ahead. That is, if Jimmy… Sir James can spare you."

Sir James nodded, and Fainworthy headed for the path leading up to Bellevue Farm.

Sir James, turning to Higgins, asked, "Are you settling on the island, sir?"

"That's right," Higgins answered. "Building a hardware and dry goods store. Hoping to see a nice little community develop here."

"Are you new to British Columbia?"

"Never been there," said Higgins.

Sir James drew himself up more stiffly, a thing that might not have seemed possible, and said, "I have the honor, sir, to inform you that you are there at this moment."

"I'm afraid I don't understand," said Higgins.

"You are on British soil, sir. And foreigners are prohibited from engaging in commerce wthout the permission of Her Majesty's government."

Griffin sighed and said, "Well, I've heard all the verses of this old song before. McGregor, I'll see you later. Jimmy, come on up to the farm whenever you want to and have a little something."

Griffin turned and walked back up the path to the farm.

Sir James, turning to McGregor, asked, "Where did this lumber come from?"

"From right here on this island," McGregor said.

"Then," said Sir James, "it will have to be confiscated, since it was stolen from the Crown."

Minerva Higgins gasped.

Her husband's lower jaw dropped open.

Zeke and Tubby stopped coiling the ropes they had just dragged free of the lumber and looked concerned.

Clarence, now standing atop the load of lumber, hunkered down instinctively.

"No stolen about it!" shouted McGregor. "I've got a permit!"

"You are a British subject, then?"

"I'm a Scot and a McGregor!"

"Then you are a British subject."

"Aye, I do bear that misfortune."

"But you," Sir James continued, turning to Higgins, "are not, I take it, a British subject."

"I'm an American citizen. And I've been given to understand that this is American soil. And I've bought this lumber from Mister McGregor, all fair and square."

"Then," said Sir James with no hint of goodwill, "I will be able to authorize the sale as soon as the export tax is paid."

"Are ye daft, man?" asked McGregor. "This timber never left the island from seed to sawmill, and it's not leavin' now!"

"I will attempt to make the situation clear even to you," said Sir James. "You, who profess to be a British subject," (Sir James ignored the ancient Celtic nonverbal expression of disgust from McGregor) "cut this timber on British soil under authority of a British permit. And you propose to sell it to an American who plans to use it on what he regards as American soil."

Higgins looked blankly at him.

McGregor said, "I've already sold it to him. And I don't give a damn what kind of soil he uses it on."

Sir James continued: "But it might interest you to know that an export tax must be paid when the merchandise passes from British to American hands. I should think five hundred dollars would be fair."

Higgins gasped.

"Fair? I paid less than a hundred dollars for it!"

"The tax would be paid by Mister McGregor, the exporter. He might, of course, choose to include that amount in the bill he submits to you."

"But he's already paid me, man!" exclaimed McGregor. "And my whole mill ain't worth five hundred dollars!"

"To save you the necessity of traveling to Victoria to pay the tax," Sir James said, "I will direct our Collector of Customs to call here at his earliest convenience. On you," he said to McGregor, "regarding payment of the export tax, and on you," he said to Higgins, "regarding payment of the necessary fees to be licensed to do business here."

Minerva Higgins stepped forward to confront Sir James: "My husband will not be answerable to a foreign customs collector or any other foreign official. You'd better have your man call on the American authorities."

Sir James stepped back and, with a slow, sweeping gesture at their surroundings, said, "Permit me to point out that there are no American authorities here."

In what might have been considered the drawing room of the Bellevue Farm manager's house, Mary and Fainworthy stood uncomfortably pretending to be at ease. After a long moment of silence, they both started to speak at once and then laughed uneasily.

"I beg your pardon, Miss Griffin. You were saying?"

"I really must apologize for…" She finished the sentence with an apologetic nod to their surroundings.

"No apology necessary, I assure you. Out in this… well, one might almost say *wilderness*… one must accept a certain shortage of amenities."

Mary sighed and said, "Including style and decor, I'm afraid."

"But, Miss Griffin, permit me to say that you bring more than sufficient style and… if I may add… decor to any room."

Mary smiled politely.

The opening and closing of the front door and heavy footsteps in the hallway announced the arrival of Griffin, who glanced into the drawing room and then entered, saying, "You should be outdoors on a fine day like this. Silly to stay cooped up in here."

"What would we do if we were outdoors, Uncle Charles?"

Griffin said, "Why, you might… er… that is to say… well, as for myself, I intend to take a pint of beer out to the kitchen garden and keep it company in one of those chairs under the cedar tree."

Mary blushed and turned away from Fainworthy, saying softly to her uncle, "The kitchen garden? Wouldn't that be a more appropriate gathering place for the servants?"

"We don't have any of what you'd call servants. But

we do have a jolly good shade tree with some comfortable chairs under it."

At the sound of the front gate opening, Griffin looked out the window and added, "By Jove, here's young Cutler. I don't suppose he'll turn down a seat in the shade and a little something wet to go with it."

"No," Mary agreed, "I'm sure he won't."

Griffin opened the front door as Cutler reached the porch.

"Come in, my dear fellow."

At the same time, Sir James came into view approaching the gate from the lower path.

"And Jimmy," said Griffin. "Come on in, both of you. We'll just go out back and make ourselves comfortable. Jimmy, this is Mister Cutler, my… er… new neighbor." Indicating Sir James, he added, "Sir James Douglas. Don't call him *Jimmy*. I keep forgetting, but he doesn't like it."

"Wouldn't think of it," said Cutler, extending his hand. "Glad to meet you, Sir James."

Sir James reluctantly shook Cutler's hand, then asked, "May I inquire, sir, if you happen to be a British subject?"

"Yep."

Griffin, startled, said, "What?"

"Yep, he can inquire." To Sir James: "Nope, I'm not a British subject."

"Then," said Sir James with the enhanced sense of dignity that accompanied his dealings with Americans, "it would interest me to learn how you came to be Mister Griffin's neighbor. This island is part of British Columbia."

"Well, there seems to be some question about that," Cutler replied. "I kinda think I'm an American homesteader on American land. A little embarrassing, though, planting my spuds where I did."

Griffin and Cutler both chuckled.

"And where was that?" Sir James asked.

"Just up the trail a ways. Had a cabin built and half my spuds planted before I found out Mister Griffin here used that land as one of his sheep runs."

"Do you mean to say you've had the audacity to settle on Hudson's Bay Company property?" demanded Sir James. To Griffin he said, "And you consider it humorous?"

"Yes," answered Griffin. "By gad, I do. Dashed humorous."

"I want this fellow and his cabin and his *spuds* removed immediately."

"Don't give me that look, Jimmy. Not my line of country, you know, removing people and cabins and spuds and all that sort of thing."

"I would like to speak with Mister Fainworthy."

"Can't think why. Pretty much of a young poop, if you ask me. But all right."

Turning toward the open door, Griffin shouted back down the hallway, "Fainworthy!"

Fainworthy hurried out of the drawing room into the

entry hall. Mary followed as far as the drawing room doorway.

Sir James said to Fainworthy, "We will return to Victoria immediately."

"Yes, Sir James." To Mary, Fainworthy said, "Miss Griffin, I'm afraid…I can't…that is, I hope I may be permitted to call on you again."

In a distraught voice, Mary said, "I should enjoy it very much."

"Thank you. For the moment, then…" (Fainworthy bowed) "your obedient servant."

Fainworthy picked his way between Griffin and Cutler, and he and Sir James turned toward the gate. As they walked, Sir James said, "I want you to find a man of spirit. One who knows the ropes. One who knows how to deal with Yankees. You will have him sworn in as a Stipendiary Magistrate…"

"Bad show," muttered Griffin as he motioned for Cutler to come into the house. "It looks as if Jimmy's about to go and put his foot in it properly this time."

Mary stepped back into the drawing room followed by Griffin and Cutler.

"Have a seat, my boy," said Griffin, plopping down in a comfortable chair and indicating another beside it. As Cutler sat, Griffin took a cigar from a box on the small table between their chairs and offered one to Cutler.

Mary, still standing, said sternly, "Uncle Charles."

"Eh. Oh, you, too, my dear. Have a seat by all means."

"Uncle Charles, do you consider it quite proper to smoke in a lady's presence? Wouldn't you prefer to take your cigar out to that chair in the kitchen garden?"

Griffin returned the cigar to the box and stood up.

Cutler stood up, too.

"Now that you mention it, no" Griffin said. "I would prefer to take a pint of beer out to a chair in the jolly old kitchen garden. Come along, my boy."

As Griffin led the way out of the drawing room, Cutler nodded to Mary and said, "Nice to have seen you again, Miss Griffin. Your obedient servant…whatever that means."

Mary Griffin stood in the doorway of the drawing room at Bellevue Farm watching Marlene coach Joe in the techniques of buttling.

Joe was dressed with obvious discomfort in an outdated cut-away frock coat, vest, and trousers that Charles Griffin would have recognized as garments which he had consigned to a trunk several years previously with the hope that he would never have to wear them again.

Joe's arms hung at his sides, and a silver tray hung from one of his hands.

"No, no," Marlene said. "You hold it like this."

She took the tray from Joe's hand and slid it between his rib cage and his upper arm.

Joe cooperated by clamping his upper arm against his side with his hands still hanging down.

"No, no," Marlene said again. "You hold it in place with your hand."

She reached down for his hand and moved it into position to hold the tray. He looked like a nervous, overdressed rugby player about to run with the ball.

"Now," she continued, "when you hear a knock at the door…"

"It really is a pity that Uncle Charles has never had a bell installed," Mary observed. "Or at least a knocker," she added.

Marlene glanced at her employer, then continued to Joe: "When you hear a knock, you go to the door and open it. And you say…?"

"Good morning," said Joe.

Marlene gestured for him to continue.

"Oh, right. Sir."

Again Marlene signalled for more. At Joe's confused expression, she hinted, "Or?"

"Oh, right. Or madam."

"And if it isn't morning?"

"Good afternoon. Sir. Or madam."

"Or?"

Joe thought intently for a moment, then said, "Or good evening. Sir or madam."

Marlene released a deep sigh and said, "And then?"

"And then ask them to come in."

"And then take the visitor's card to Miss Griffin. Or whoever the person is here to see. All right, let's try it."

Mary stepped aside. Marlene went into the hall,

opened the front door, went out and closed it behind her.

When three knocks sounded, a hesitant look appeared on Joe's face.

"Answer the door, Joe," Mary said.

Joe took a few steps toward the front door, then turned back to say, "Yes, Miss," before continuing. He pulled the door open and stood looking at Marlene. She gestured for him to proceed.

"Good morning. Sir or madam."

At a deep sigh from behind him, Joe turned and looked at Mary. A smile flickered across Marlene's face but was gone by the time Joe turned back toward her.

"*Either* sir *or* madam," Marlene explained. "Not both. Well, go on."

"Come inside."

"*Please* come inside," said Marlene.

"But I'm already…oh, I get you. *Please* come inside."

Mary said, "It would help if you stepped back so she *could* come inside."

Joe stepped back, and Marlene came inside. She nodded toward the door, and when Joe had closed it she said, "Is Miss Griffin at home?"

"Well, sure she is." Joe pointed down the hall at Mary.

Marlene shook her head in despair and explained, "A visitor would ask if Miss Griffin was at home. And then you would take the visitor's card and give it to her."

Marlene held a card out to Joe, who took it in his free

hand and started to turn away with the empty tray still tucked under his arm.

"No, no, no. You use the tray to carry the card."

Joe took the tray out from under his arm, placed the card on it, and started to take it to Mary.

"No!" moaned Marlene. "Here's how you hold the tray."

She took the tray in one hand and, with her other hand, pulled and twisted Joe's hand into the correct palm-up position. Then she placed the tray on it.

"And you don't take the card from the visitor," she went on. "You hold the tray out to the visitor. The visitor puts the card on the tray. You take the card to Miss Griffin on the tray. Here, give it back."

Joe handed the card back. Immediately Marlene held it out again, and Joe extended the tray to receive the card.

Then, as Joe continued to stand at the door, Mary said, "I'm at home, Joe, and waiting to find out who my visitor is."

"Well, it's…" Joe pointed to Marlene. "Oh, I get you."

He walked to Mary with the tray extended, then took the card from the tray with his other hand and held it out to her.

Marlene stalked to where they stood, snatched the card from Mary's hand, stalked back to the front door, yanked it open, and slammed it behind her.

Mary said softly, "You're supposed to let me pick it up from the tray."

Joe nodded in a spirit of cooperation which contained

no element of comprehension.

The three knocks on the door were repeated. Mary gestured for Joe to answer it. He went to the door, opened it, and found Fainworthy standing there. Marlene had stepped down off the porch and was watching from the walk that led out to the gate.

"Is Miss Griffin at home?" inquired Fainworthy.

"Good morning. Sir. Or…well…sir. Please come inside."

Joe stepped back, then remembered to extend the tray. He accomplished this by first extending his hand palm up toward Fainworthy and then placing the tray on his hand. Fainworthy produced a card case from an inner pocket, removed a card, and dropped it onto the tray. Joe turned to discover that Mary was no longer in the hallway.

"She was here just a minute ago," he said. He walked down the hall, shifted the tray to his other hand, gripping it by the edge, saw Mary in the room, went in and thrust the tray at her.

"Not like that," Mary said. "Here's how you do it."

Mary took the tray, balanced it on an upturned hand, walked gracefully out into the hallway, saw Fainworthy, and almost dropped the tray.

"Mister Fainworthy. I didn't know…here, Joe, come and take this tray!"

Joe came into the hallway and took the tray as Marlene came in through the front door.

To Fainworthy, Mary explained, "I'm trying to train a household staff."

"I understand, Miss Griffin." Smiling, he added, "Not to put too fine a point on it, you're attempting to make a silk purse out of…"

"Exactly." To Marlene: "Potts, take Joe out to the kitchen and try to teach him how to handle the various items of a dinner service. And see how those housemaids are getting on."

"Yes, Miss. Come along, Joe."

They left through a door at the back of the hall as Fainworthy followed Mary into the drawing room.

"Permit me to say, Miss Griffin, that you're looking exceedingly well this morning."

"Thank you, Mister Fainworthy. Won't you sit down?"

Mary sat on a small sofa, leaving room for Fainworthy to sit beside her, but he sat on a chair facing her.

Mary said, "I'm so glad you were able to call again. I'm afraid your official duties demand a large part of your time."

"One does, perhaps, find precious little time for more personal pursuits."

"And yet it must be very interesting to play such an important role in the growth of the Empire."

"Oh, well, I can hardly claim to play a major role. Of course, one does one's part as best one can."

The sound of the front door opening and closing was followed by the sound of Griffin's voice in the hallway:

"Mary! Has that young poop Fai..."

Griffin appeared in the drawing room doorway and stopped.

"Oh. Ah. Mister Fainworthy. When you go back to Victoria, tell Jimmy..."

Fainworthy winced.

"All right, tell *Sir James* that Wilson has another batch of smoked hams ready for delivery."

"I shall give him that message the moment I return to Victoria."

"You'll want to leave immediately, I assume."

"Of course. Perhaps, Miss Griffin, you would do me the honor of walking with me as far as the gate."

"Of course," she replied, and they went out together.

As they walked toward the gate, Mary said, "I must thank you again for doing me the honor of calling on me. I'm sure the young ladies in Victoria must simply fight for your attention. Or has one of them already claimed you?"

"I am quite unattached, Miss Griffin. I may say, however, that very recently I have begun to develop feelings warmer and deeper than those of ordinary friendship for a most charming young lady..."

"Morning, Miss Griffin!" called Cutler from the path. "Fainworthy. Nice to see you again."

As the couple quickly moved away from each other, Cutler added cheerfully, "Why, Fainworthy, you dog.

Pitchin' a little woo? Sorry I interrupted."

"Not at all. Or, rather, nothing to…" To Mary: "I'll try to get back out here later in the week. That is to say, I think certain matters will require my attention. May I call on you at that time?"

"Yes. Please do."

Cutler swung open the gate, saying, "Don't leave on my account. I'm just here to see Mister Griffin for a minute."

Mary said, "I believe you'll find him in the house."

"Thanks. Be seeing you, Fainworthy."

Fainworthy, not quite bowing, replied, "Your servant, sir."

As Cutler stepped up onto the porch, Fainworthy bowed and said, "Miss Griffin… Mary… your most devoted servant." Then he passed through the gate and down the path.

Mary cast an annoyed glance at Cutler's back as he entered the house snickering.

~ 7 ~

The word *evening* carries a variety of connotations. In its most general sense, it refers to the period between dinnertime and bedtime. More specifically, it may designate the period of daylight that remains after dinnertime, which makes it virtually meaningless during the winter months when darkness falls during the preparation of the "evening" meal. Socially, a specific hour is often chosen as the beginning of *evening*, which by implication becomes *night* when someone goes home or goes to bed.

The sun's progress down the sky toward the horizon and the fading light that remains in the sky after sundown provide a pleasantly vague alternative to establishing, or even caring, when afternoon becomes evening and evening becomes night.

In the late spring and early summer, which is the season when most people think and talk about *evening* if they ever think and talk about it at all, the word has little practical meaning in the vicinity of the San Juan Islands. Outdoor activities can be done in full daylight for two hours or more after dinner. The lightness of the post-sundown sky seems to justify allowing children to play outdoors beyond their normal bedtime. The very slow fading of the light allows couples an additional hour or so to stroll alone, away from prying eyes, to an extent that might be slightly scandalous after dark; at least, it might have been slightly scandalous in 1859.

On this particular evening in early summer, the sun was below the horizon. The overhead illumination was bright enough for Cutler and Marlene to walk aimlessly across the grassy open ground of Bellevue Farm and up the hill toward the wild rose bushes bordering Cutler's potato patch without stepping in an unseen dip or stumbling over an unseen rock. At ground level, though, the light had that soft, elusive quality often described as "romantic".

"Thank you ever so much for helping me with those carpets," Marlene said. "I'm sure I'd still be there whacking away if I'd had to do them myself."

"Glad I could help. Besides, there's better things to do than spend all night beating carpets."

"Not that beating carpets is rightly a part of my duties. But I like to oblige when I can. How was I to know the girl I was helping would have to go and help the cook?"

Cutler put an arm around her waist. She willingly

moved closer to him.

Looking into her eyes, he said, "You know, you have the most beautiful eyes. They're like…"

The sounds of snorting and snuffling from the other side of the bushes intruded on what had promised to be a tender moment, although they may have saved Cutler from uttering one of the more overworked conclusions to that simile.

"That pig!" Cutler blurted.

"What!" Marlene moved abruptly away from him.

"That damned pig is in my spuds again!"

Cutler shoved his way through a gap near the uphill end of the bushes. Marlene watched him in exasperation and then walked down the slope to the path that curved past Cutler's place on its way down from the hilltop to Bellevue Farm and the waterfront. As she reached the path, she nearly collided with Griffin, who had been leisurely smoking a cigar when he heard Cutler's outburst and was hurrying to investigate.

Marlene followed Griffin up the path and around the bushes, where they found Cutler snatching up small rocks. He was winding up to throw one at the pig when Griffin exclaimed, "I say! How did Caesar get loose again?"

Cutler lowered his throwing arm, saying, "I don't know. But I wish you'd keep your pig out of my potatoes."

"You ought to put up a fence. Only sensible thing to do. Up to you, don't you know, to keep your potatoes out of my pig."

Griffin chuckled and said, "Rather good, that: pig out of potatoes, potatoes out of pig, I mean to say, what?"

Griffin, still chuckling at his inadvertent witticism, began prodding and nudging the pig with his walking stick, guiding it to the path and back down toward the farm.

"You coming, Miss Potts?"

Marlene and Cutler exchanged a pair of rapid looks expressing remorse, disappointment, and hope for the future before she answered: "Oh. Yes."

As she followed Griffin down the path, Cutler systematically hurled each of his rocks against the trunk of the tree beside his cabin, where each successive *thunk* made him wish more fervently that he could hear them *thunking* against the side of the pig.

~ 8 ~

Tubby and Higgins were holding a long piece of siding against the frame of the new store as Zeke and Clarence nailed it to the studs. Two steam whistles blasting simultaneously, one an irritating half-tone higher than the other, drew their attention toward the water.

The *Beaver* and the *Sylvia* were entering the bay from opposite directions. They glided silently toward the pier; and as they arrived within a few feet of it, deckhands jumped across the intervening water holding mooring lines which they secured to the bull rail.

Cutler strolled down the path and stopped to admire the progress on the store. English and American farm wives, some accompanied by children, came down the road and out onto the pier to hand in or receive mail for themselves and their neighbors.

Sam Pike stepped off the *Beaver*'s gangplank just as Ike

Webster stepped down from the *Sylvia*'s cargo door. They shook hands, laughed, and came ashore. They were still laughing when Cutler came to join them.

"What are you fellas doing out here?" he asked. "And what's so funny?"

Pike said, "I went over to Victoria like I said we oughta do, and a fancy-pants Englishman that works for the Governor gave me a job as a Stipendiary Magistrate. Wrote me out a certificate, paid me a month's stipend in advance, and sent me out here."

"To do what?"

"To collect a five-hundred-dollar export tax on a hundred bucks worth of lumber that never left the island."

Webster said, "And I was swapping lies with Barney Ellis...he's the Sheriff over in Whatcom now...when he got word of what they were sending Sam out here to do. He was bound and determined to swear in a special deputy to come out here and arrest him as a common offender. I talked myself into the job, thinking that's the best way to keep things from getting out of hand."

Cutler laughed and said, "Looks like it'll take some finagling to smooth this over."

"Got any ideas as to just how that finagling's gonna work?" asked Pike.

"Not at the moment," admitted Cutler. "But we'll think of something."

"And what do we do in the meantime?" asked Webster.

"Get to know the lay of the land. Meet the people. Do a little socializing."

"And we're gonna to that exactly how?" inquired Pike.

"By going to a barn dance."

Another of those long summer evenings had reached the point where even people who took such things for granted were inclined to notice and enjoy the drawn-out ending of the day. There was the slightly unvirtuous pleasure of indulging in recreation while there was still plenty of light for plowing, washing clothes, splitting wood, and any number of other important tasks. And, as the skylight finally began to dim perceptibly, there was the impending start of a social event that would last until well after dark.

Bellevue Farm's big barn had been emptied of animals and farm equipment. It had been swept and scrubbed. Dozens of lanterns had been hung from the beams. English and American farm wives had laid out food on long tables while their husbands had superintended the two-man job of setting up a huge beer keg.

Now the children playing among the shadows in the barn and among the farm implements outside were summoned to the pump beside the open main door to have their hands and faces washed preparatory to converging on their own food table. The men who had supervised the setting up of the beer keg now took part in the testing of the results. Zeke, Tubby, and Clarence had unpacked, respectively, a fiddle, a harmonica, and a concertina and were about to play.

Cutler, Webster, and Pike walked down the hill behind the farm and across the grassy field to join the growing population around the barn's main entrance. After exchanging a few greetings and participating in a few introductions, they sidestepped the children swarming around the pump, smiled at the ladies in charge of the hands-and-faces-washing project, and entered the barn.

Griffin stood near the main door, clearly enjoying the activity. Mary stood beside him, clearly not sharing his enjoyment. Marlene stood a few steps behind Mary, clearly enjoying it enough for both of them.

"Glad you could make, it," Griffin called to Cutler. "Thought you might be out playing hide and seek with my pig again."

Griffin laughed, Cutler smiled, Webster and Pike looked amiably bewildered. Mary flushed with embarrassment.

"Mister Griffin has a pig that seems fond of my spuds," Cutler explained to his friends. "He and I have different notions of what to do about it."

"Young Cutler here thinks I should keep my pig out of his potatoes," Griffin began with a roguish smile.

"Oh, Uncle Charles…" Mary began.

"But," Griffin continued, "I say he needs to build a fence and keep his potatoes out of my pig."

Pike and Webster joined the round of laughter at this witticism which Mary hadn't thought highly of the first, second, or third time she'd heard it.

"Ever been to a barn dance before?" asked Cutler, including both Mary and Marlene in his inquiry.

Marlene smiled but refrained from answering, knowing that Cutler's inclusion of herself and her employer in the same conversation would be taken by Mary as a violation of etiquette and that to respond would be taken as impertinence.

"No," Mary replied.

"Didn't want to come," said her uncle. "Blurring the social order, she calls it."

"Please, Uncle Charles."

"I told her we're democratic out here. No ruddy aristocrats, by gad."

"Speaking of no aristocrats," Cutler said, "I want you to meet my old prospecting partners, Ike Webster and Sam Pike. Gents, meet Miss Potts and Miss Griffin. And Mister Griffin, who runs this farm."

As they exchanged suitable acknowledgements, the musicians erupted in a lively tune.

Webster promptly asked, "Miss Potts, can I have the pleasure of this dance?"

Cutler darted a look of displeasure at him as Marlene, with a brief rueful smile at Cutler, said, "Delighted, I'm sure" and allowed Webster to lead her to the section of the barn which had been designated as the dance floor.

Cutler said, "Miss Griffin? Would you care to dance?"

"Oh, I don't really think I …"

"Don't be silly, my dear," said Griffin. "Go shake a leg and have some fun."

Cutler extended an arm to Mary. Good breeding overcame her reluctance, and she placed a hand on his arm, prepared to be led elegantly to the dance floor. Instead, Cutler flung his other arm around her waist and whisked her away in a high-stepping frontier polka.

Across the barn, Higgins stood watching as his wife assisted in setting out plates, silverware, mugs, and pitchers of punch. He was, perhaps, unconsciously intrigued by the spectacle of her performing in an active rather than a supervisory role.

In any case, he soon lost interest and wandered away, aimlessly skirting the fringes of the crowd.

"Mister Higgins!" Griffin called to him. "Someone here you ought to meet."

Higgins instantly brightened up and went to join Griffin and Pike.

"Always glad to meet another neighbor," he said.

"Not exactly a neighbor," Pike said. "But I may be around from time to time. Sam Pike."

"Norbert Higgins. Hardware and dry goods. Pleased to meet you."

They shook hands.

Meanwhile, Mary was maintaining the obligatory pleasant if slightly rigid facial expression as she was whirled around the dance floor. Somehow, though, the effort to get in step with her partner and to adjust to, if not anticipate, his moves was apparently somewhat enjoyable: a close observer might have caught an actual smile on her face from time to time.

Marlene, while new to the North American barn dance, was no stranger to lively dancing in general and thoroughly enjoyed her whirlwind tour around the central part of the barn with Webster.

When the music ended, it left Mary breathless but smiling with Cutler's arm still around her waist. She regained her composure as they returned to where Webster and Marlene had rejoined Griffin, Pike, and Higgins.

Webster was saying to Marlene, "You kept up with me real good out there. When they start up again, how 'bout…"

Cutler said, "Ike, I need to talk to you a minute" and led Webster a few steps away.

"There's lots of women here you can dance with," Cutler went on.

"That's right," his friend agreed. "Including Marlene, if I want to."

"Well, she's having the next dance with me."

They were about to debate the point when the musicians launched another lively tune, and Cutler and Webster quickly turned to see Pike leading Marlene to the dance floor. Cutler glared. Webster grinned. Then they both laughed and rejoined Griffin, Higgins, and Mary.

"Caught your breath yet?" Cutler asked Mary.

"I think so."

"Care to try it again?"

"I think so. Yes."

"Then let's go kick a few shins."

This time Mary stepped easily into his embrace, and they careened out into the maelstrom of dancers whose enthusiasm, which greatly exceeded their skill, made the experience all the more adventurous.

Just as evening lingers long in the San Juan Islands in the summer, morning comes, in some people's opinion, prematurely. Early risers accustomed to starting their day in darkness during the winter and rising literally with the sun at other seasons may enjoy the fact that, in the summer, the sky is already bright by the time they spring from their beds. But one who disdains the "early to rise" portion of the old saying after having ignored the "early to bed" portion the night before may find it difficult to catch those extra few winks he needs in order to be at his best for the new day. He may be certain that the local bird population has trebled overnight and that each individual bird has been taught to chirp or warble through a megaphone. He may curse the sun for consulting its compass and sextant in order to find the precise angle to pierce his bedroom window and shine directly on his eyelids.

The effort, almost always unsuccessful, to overcome these hardships and drift back into slumber has been known to make even a usually good-natured personality just a bit peevish.

It was so on the morning after the barn dance. The sun, probing systematically down the wall of Cutler's cabin, found the window. Entering, it appeard to take no interest in Pike and Webster in their bedrolls on the floor. But it found Cutler, in his union suit, moving restlessly on the bed, already disturbed by the music festival being held by the birds.

A snuffling sound that might have gone undetected by a sounder sleeper caught Cutler's ear. He lay still and listened intently. A familiar snort from his potato patch brought him jumping off the bed and stumbling to the door.

Griffin's pig was rooting among the potatoes. Cutler ran out into the garden, waving his arms in the most threatening manner possible. His efforts were in vain, mostly because the aspect of the pig which was most directly presented to his view was not its face. Dancing sideways over the cultivated ground, he continued to jump and wave as he maneuvered to get within the pig's range of vision.

When the pig finally noticed Cutler, it gave him a blank stare and then resumed its meal.

In his efforts to attract the pig's attention, Cutler had

failed to notice Marlene standing on the path behind him; but when he now supplemented his physical antics with the vocalization alluded to on a previous occasion, her burst of laughter got his attention.

    Cutler whirled around, glared at Marlene, then glanced down at himself standing barefoot among his potatoes in his union suit. With men, embarrassment may bring the blush of shame; but it also brings, in most cases, vigorous and often shortsighted and unfortunate action. A few quick steps took Cutler to the open door of his cabin. A quick reach through the doorway procured his Kentucky rifle. In an instant, he pivoted, took aim at the pig, and fired.

    The pig flopped to the ground. Marlene screamed and hurried away down the path. Cutler lowered his rifle and muttered, "Damn. Looks like Jimmy's not the only one that's gone and put his foot in it."

An hour later, Griffin and Fainworthy were seated in the two most comfortable chairs of the Bellevue Farm drawing room. Griffin took a cigar from the box on the table between them, then turned the box toward Fainworthy.

"Thank you, no," said Fainworthy. "I never smoke in the morning."

Griffin shook his head in amusement, then said, "I'd never smoke at all if my niece had her... that is to say, of course I only smoke when she's not here. Not proper to smoke in front of a lady, she tells me."

Griffin clipped the end off his cigar, rolled the cigar between his palms, and then lighted it.

Fainworthy said, "As for Miss Griffin coming to Victoria for the concerts, Sir James assures me that he and Lady Douglas will deem it an honor to have her stay with them."

Griffin savored his cigar before saying, "For a week, you say."

"If you could permit her to be away that long."

"Oh, absolutely."

Griffin exhaled contentedly and then reconsidered the implications of his enthusiastic approval.

"That is to say, I'll miss her like the dickens, of course, and all that sort of thing. But naturally she misses the social life. Yes, yes, take her to Victoria by all means."

A knock at the front door was followed by heavy footsteps in the hall. A moment later, Joe entered the drawing room carrying the empty tray as if it held a calling card.

"Well?" asked Griffin.

"Lyman Cutler is here to see you," said Joe. "Sir."

"Well, bring him in," said Griffin. "And then you can go back to…whatever you do these days."

Joe went out, and a moment later Cutler came in.

Griffin motioned Cutler to a seat on the sofa, saying, "Good morning, my boy. I think you know Fainworthy here."

Cutler, nodding, said, "Morning, Fainworthy."

Fainworthy nodded less perceptibly and responded, "Mister Cutler."

As Cutler sat, Griffin held out the cigar box.

"No, thanks. I'm sorry to butt in, but I've got to talk to you."

"Certainly, my dear fellow. What's the trouble?"

"I've shot your pig," said Cutler, "and I've come to pay you for it."

Fainworthy jumped to his feet saying, "What?"

Griffin said, "Shot my pig? What on earth did you do that for?"

"He was in my spuds again, and I was half asleep, and…well…"

"And so you potted him? By gad!"

"I'm sorry I did it, and I'm here to pay up. Will ten dollars cover it?"

Griffin said, "I accept your apology, but Caesar was a prize breeding boar. He was worth easily twenty-five dollars."

"I could buy a pig like that down on Puget Sound for ten dollars any day," Cutler said. "But I was wrong to shoot him, and if twenty-five dollars is your price, then I'll pay it. I'll have to owe you for most of it, though, until I can sell my spuds."

Fainworthy said, "The price is one hundred dollars."

Cutler jumped to his feet saying, "Are you crazy?"

Griffin stood up less abruptly and said, "He certainly wasn't worth anything like a hundred dollars."

Unseen by Cutler, Mary entered the room.

Griffin quickly and guiltily put out his cigar.

Fainworthy, assuming his most self-important pose, said, "One hundred dollars, Mister Cutler. Payble immediately. Sir James has honored me with the authority to say that failure to remit payment of any moneys owed to the Crown, the Hudson's Bay Company, or any person living on British soil will carry the most dire consequences."

Cutler took a step toward Fainworthy, saying, "How'd you like me to show you some dire consequences?"

Fainworthy took two quick steps backward; or, to be more accurate, one of his feet took a quick step backward and the other foot, which had been assigned to take the second step, collided with his chair with the result that his body continued backward and Fainworthy resumed his sitting position in a manner entirely unsuited to his dignity.

Mary gasped.

Cutler turned to her, instantly apologetic.

"Sorry, Miss Griffin. Didn't mean to cause any trouble. Mister Griffin, if you don't mind, I'll settle up with you later."

Griffin, Fainworthy, and Mary watched Cutler leave the room and heard the front door open and close before Fainworthy, rising again, said, "I regret that you had to witness a scene like that, Miss Griffin. However, one must be forceful with these fellows. Now, if you will excuse me…"

"Are you going after him?" Mary inquired.

Griffin said, "Not if he's got an ounce more brain than a cuckoo clock."

"I am sailing immediately for Victoria. I shall return with a warrant for that fellow's arrest."

"Not one of your brainier schemes, young fellow," Griffin told him. "I should think he'd offer resistance, don't you know."

"I shall have a squad of armed men with me."

Griffin smiled broadly.

Mary looked embarrassed on Fainworthy's behalf.

"Merely as a formality," Fainworthy continued. "To show him that we mean business. Not that I...er...wouldn't be quite willing to handle the matter myself."

Fainworthy bowed stiffly in Mary's direction, then went out.

~ 10 ~

The Whatcom waterfront was as busy as ever. Cutler, Zeke, McGregor, and Tubby left the *Sylvia*, went ashore, and walked up the hill into the town.

Where the first side street angled off from the main route, they separated. Cutler and Zeke entered the gunsmith's shop. McGregor went on to the hardware store, which advertised mining supplies, and went inside. Tubby continued further up the hill and went into the general store.

A few minutes later, Cutler and Zeke left the gunsmith's shop, Cutler carrying a small sack and Zeke with a small keg of gunpowder on his shoulder.

McGregor rejoined them from the hardware store with a spool of uncut fuse material tucked under his arm.

Tubby returned from the general store carrying a

rolled-up object tied with twine near each end. Its red and white stripes proclaimed it to be an American flag.

Satisfied with their purchases, the four men walked back down to the pier and out to the *Sylvia*.

On the open ground above the bluff near Bellevue Farm, Zeke and Tubby tamped down the dirt and rocks around the flagpole they had just erected. Then Higgins fastened the American flag to the pole's halyard, hoisted the flag, and secured the rope to a wooden cleat.

Nearby, American settlers and English farmhands mixed gunpowder with other granular substances in buckets.

At an improvised table, farm wives cut heavy paper into smaller pieces and formed the pieces into tubes. Others inserted a thin wooden disk into one end of each tube before passing it to Clarence and McGregor, who filled the tubes with the various gunpowder mixtures and attached lengths of fuse material. Each tube was then passed to another woman who sealed the open end with a paper disk.

Another table held several metal pipes of varying lengths, an assortment of springs, and some tools. Beside them, Jeremiah Long dumped gun parts from the sack Cutler had brought from Whatcom and began test-fitting them to the metal tubes.

Children of American and English settlers played together as their mothers laid out picnic lunches.

Across the path, in the front yard of the farmhouse, Charles Griffin tended a pig roasting on a spit.

In the harbor below, the *Beaver* was tied up at the pier. Fainworthy left the pier followed by Alf, Tom, Will, and Jack shouldering their rifles.

As the procession approached the level ground, Fainworthy glared at the American flag and the festive activity going on around it. As he and the marines reached the front gate of Bellevue Farm, Fainworthy demanded of Griffin, "Don't you have a Union Jack?"

"I seem to think maybe I do. Somewhere," Griffin said.

"Find it and put it up."

"Haven't got a flagpole to run it up on. I say, though, McGregor could come up with something. Dashed capable feller, McGregor."

Fainworthy almost spat out the name "McGregor." Then: "Claims to be a British subject, and there he is fraternizing with those Yankees. Never trust a Scotsman."

Griffin couldn't suppress a smile as he said, "No more than they should trust us, eh?"

His smile faded quickly under the pressure of Fainworthy's scowl.

"Find that flag," Fainworthy ordered, "and get it up… with no help from McGregor. I'm going up to arrest that fellow Cutler."

Fainworthy strode off up the path followed by the marines, who looked enviously at the preparations being made all around them.

"Pushy young devil," Griffin complained to no one in particular as he crossed to the porch.

As he reached for the doorknob, the door opened and Mary came out.

"Now, don't you touch anything with those greasy fingers," she said.

"Oh. Certainly not, my dear."

He started to lick his fingers.

"Uncle Charles!"

"Eh? Oh." He lowered his hands and tried to wipe them surreptitiously on his pants legs.

"Really, Uncle Charles!"

"Sorry, my dear."

"What do you want?"

"A little peace and quiet in my own home," he said; but he said it silently. Aloud, he said, "I want that little Union Jack that's on the top shelf under the stairs. At least I think that's where it is. And something to use for a flag pole. A broom handle or something, don't you know."

"I'll get them and bring them to you."

"Very kind of you, my dear. Thank you. And some

string or rope or something."

"All right. Now go back and tend your pig."

Griffin returned to the fire pit and tended his pig.

Soon Mary came back out of the house carrying a small flag, a broom, and a ball of twine.

"Thank you, my dear," Griffin said. He took the flag from Mary and, without thinking, started to wipe his greasy hands on it.

"Uncle Charles!"

"Eh? Oh, by Jove! Bad show, what?"

He thrust the flag back into Mary's hands, licked his fingers, wiped them on his pants legs, then took the twine and the broom from her. Mary draped the flag over the fence and returned to the house.

Griffin took out his pocket knife and cut several lengths of twine. Then he ran the twine through grommets in the flag and tied them to the broom handle. Finally he lashed the broom, bristles down and flag up, to the nearest fence post.

Fainworthy and the marines came back down the path and halted at the gate. The marines, safely behind Fainworthy's back, smiled at the improvised display of the flag. Fainworthy said to Griffin, "His cabin is empty. I don't suppose you happen to know where he might be."

At that moment, Cutler came around the side of the farmhouse carrying more wood for Griffin's fire.

"Oh, this really is too much!" blurted Fainworthy.

"Howdy, fellas," said Cutler, stopping in front of Griffin.

"Drop that wood!" commanded Fainworthy.

Cutler looked from Fainworthy to Griffin.

"Drop it, I say!"

"Right here?" Cutler asked.

"Right there! At once!"

Cutler shrugged and dropped the wood so close to Griffin's feet that Griffin stepped back, lost his balance, staggered against the fence, clutched the broom handle for support, and wrenched it loose from its moorings.

Cutler gave Griffin a hand and pulled him to his feet, saying, "Been taking dancing lessons from our friend Fainworthy here?"

Griffin and Cutler laughed; then, still laughing, Cutler picked up the broom stick and spanked the dust off the flag, which was still attached to it.

Fainworthy grabbed Alf's rifle, swiveled to take an inexpert aim across the path, and fired a shot through the American flag.

"Laugh that off, you bloody…"

Cutler darted through the gate and confronted Fainworthy on the path. Fainworthy dropped the rifle and took a few quick steps backward; fortunately for what little dignity he preserved during this action, there was nothing behind him to trip him up.

American settlers rushed toward the scene.

Cutler addressed the settlers: "It's all right, fellas. Alf

here was just letting me look at his rifle, and I accidentally dropped it and it went off. Say, Old Glory doesn't look so bad with a battle scar, now does she?"

Cutler picked up the rifle and handed it to Alf.

"Sorry, Alf. Say, Mister Griffin, how much longer on that pig?"

Griffin said, "Not more than a quarter of an hour, I should think."

"Hear that, fellas? Better start rounding up the wives and kiddies. Have the ladies start dishing up that potato salad and passing out the biscuits."

As the settlers dispersed, Zeke said to Tubby, "I've seen Lyman Cutler handle a rifle. If he dropped that one, I'm the Queen of England."

"Pleased to meet you, Your Majesty," replied Tubby. "Come on, now. We don't want any hard feelings today."

Fainworthy, regaining his composure, announced, "Mister Cutler, you're under arrest."

Cutler looked at Fainworthy with mixed hostility and bewilderment.

"I just saved your hide. I don't think you want to carry this any further, do you?"

"I said you're under arrest."

"Have it your way, then. But I'd like a witness or two." Raising his voice, he said, "Hey, fellas, gather around! Mister Fainworthy here wants to say a few words in honor of the occasion!"

The Americans turned and began to come back.

"Go ahead, Mister Fainworthy," Cutler invited. "What was it you wanted to say?"

In an undertone, Fainworthy said, "On second thought, perhaps I should consult Sir James before proceeding in this matter."

Griffin, still tending his pig on the other side of the fence, muttered, "Perhaps you jolly well should. Infernal young poop."

"My mistake, fellas!" called Cutler. "He congratulates us on the anniversary of our independence but reserves his more detailed remarks for another time!"

Fainworthy motioned abruptly to the marines and then led them down the path toward the water as the Americans cheered.

Much later that night, a bonfire burned near (but not too near) the American flagpole. American and English settlers passed jugs as they watched the home-made fireworks, launched by McGregor and Zeke from contraptions built by Jeremiah, arching into the night sky and exploding over the bay with limited visual appeal but plenty of noise.

Cutler and Marlene stood by themselves beyond the firelight overlooking the bay.

Marlene murmured, "I don't know but what this is the nicest view I ever saw."

"I know of one that's even nicer," said Cutler.

"Where's that?"

"Right here," he replied, gazing into her eyes.

"Oh. My, how you do go on, Mister Cutler."

"*Lyman*, remember?"

Cutler kissed her.

Smiling, Marlene said, "Well, have it your way: *Lyman*," and she gave him a hasty kiss in return.

Near the bonfire, Tubby started to play *My Country, 'tis of Thee* on his harmonica. A few of the American settlers began to sing the words. Then a few of the English settlers began to sing the words of *God Save the Queen*, the English song which had first made that melody familiar to Americans.

The American and English singers glanced uncertainly at each other as more singers joined each group. For a moment the singing was what might be called competitive; then both groups of singers grinned and went on happily singing their different words to the same tune.

Sam Pike stood in the morning sunlight watching Higgins and McGregor hang the sign on the front of the new store. They all turned to look as Ike Webster came half running and half stumbling down the road from beyond the wooded headland.

"What's wrong?" Higgins asked in alarm.

"That damned Englishman again?" demanded McGregor.

Webster shook his head. "Barney Ellis is here wth the County Commissioners from Whatcom."

"What for?" Pike asked.

"To auction off Bellevue Farm's livestock in lieu of back taxes."

Pike, shaking his head in despair, said. "Do they seriously expect a British company to pay American taxes?"

"I think they expect to buy livestock for themselves real cheap."

"How long till they get here?"

"They're landing now at that little beach around the point."

"Okay. You go stall 'em. I'll warn Griffin."

Webster hurried back up the road he'd just come down while Pike set a quick pace up the other path to Bellevue Farm.

On the front porch of the store, McGregor muttered, "They're all daft."

Sheriff Ellis and the County Commissioners paused at the Bellevue Farm gate with Webster taking up the rear. Then Ellis pushed the gate open and led the way past the house, through the kitchen garden, and out through another gate to the barn. When they arrived, they found Griffin, Pike, and Joe leaning casually on the fence of an empty sheep pen. Through a side door in the barn, empty cow stalls could be seen. Beyond the empty pig sty was an empty chicken coop.

Webster said to Ellis, "I still think you ought to go slow, Barney."

"I appreciate the advice, Ike. But the taxes ain't been paid, so the auction's gonna be held." To Griffin he asked, "Are you Charles Griffin?"

"That's who I am. Yes."

"I'm Sheriff Ellis. I have orders here to confiscate and auction off the livestock of this farm in lieu of unpaid taxes.

This is a copy of the order."

He held a paper out to Griffin. Griffin leaned forward, looked at the paper, then leaned back without taking it.

Ellis went on: "Where's all your livestock?"

"Open range," answered Griffin.

To the Commissioners, Ellis said, "Okay, gents. I guess the auction's off."

"You're doing the right thing, Barney," Webster said.

"Instead," continued Ellis, "it's a straight sale. A dime a head for every animal you round up."

"Now you're doing the wrong thing again, Barney," said Webster.

The Commissioners dispersed in search of animals. Webster went back to the path and turned uphill.

A milk cow, two sheep, and a goat stood at the edge of Cutler's potato patch. As two Comissioners emerged from the bushes and started trying to round them up, Cutler stepped out of his cabin holding his Kentucky rifle and said, "Mind if I ask what you fellas are up to?"

"Rounding up livestock from Bellevue Farm," one of them replied.

"We're taking them for back taxes," said the other.

"Well, these are my critters," Cutler told them, "and I'll thank you to leave 'em alone."

He squared his shoulders and rather ostentatiously brought one finger toward the trigger.

The first Commissioner said, "Our mistake. Sorry."

Both Commissioners hurried back the way they had come.

"Thanks for the tip, Ike," said Cutler without turning around.

Webster emerged from the cabin and said, "Sam and me knew we could count on your help."

In the late afternoon, Cutler, Webster, and Pike stood on the grassy tip of the wooded headland looking down at the bay. Turning their heads, they looked down on a muddy beach on the other side of the headland. On the beach, the outgoing tide had left two big flat-bottom rowboats high and dry among barnacle-encrusted rocks.

Sheriff Ellis and the County Commissioners wrangled a dozen sheep, two goats, and a pig through the trees and down to the beach.

Cutler muttered, "Git along, little dogies," and his companions smiled.

Then Pike said, "Oh, hell. Look."

He pointed across the bay to where the *Beaver* had emerged from the narrow channel between San Juan Island and Lopez Island. As it crossed the bay toward the pier, they could see Fainworthy and an augmented squad of marines on deck.

"Come on," Cutler said. "I guess we better give those rustlers a hand."

Cutler, Webster, and Pike thrashed their way through

ferns, bracken, and nettles to the muddy beach where they helped shove the boats far enough out into the water for their sterns to float free. In helping to load the animals, they succeeded in scaring half of them away. Then they unceremoniously "helped" Ellis and the Commissioners into the boats and shoved them off so vigorously that they were well away from the beach before they could get their oars unshipped.

Wading back out of the knee-deep water, Pike said, "Lyman, you better lay low. When Fainworthy finds his pigeons have flown the coop, he may take a notion to go after you again."

Webster said, "I'm not so sure he was after Barney's little posse in the first place. I think he's come back for Lyman."

"Whatever he's up to, I say Lyman oughta lay low."

"Good idea," Cutler agreed. "You fellas go stall him. I'll see you later."

Cutler picked his way through the trees toward the center of the island as Webster and Pike climbed up from the beach to the road leading around the back of the headland and down to the pier.

~13~

At Fort Steilacoom, Colonel Casey and General Harney stood facing each other across the desk.

Casey's orderly entered through the open door and stepped as far aside from Harney as he could to address Casey.

"What is it?" barked Harney.

"A gentleman to see Colonel Casey, sir. By appointment."

Casey asked, "Mister Campbell?"

"Yes, sir."

Harney said, "We don't need to see Mister…"

"Show him in," said Casey.

"Yes, sir."

The orderly backed up two steps, turned and hurried out of the office, returning a moment later ahead of Archibald Campbell. As Harney glared at both of them, the orderly hurried back out again.

Casey said, "General Harney, this is…"

"We've met," said Harney. "What do you need, Mister Campbell?"

Glancing uncertainly from Harney to Casey and back to Harney, Campbell replied, "I suppose what I need most is to dispel some rumors."

"What rumors?" Casey asked.

"Rumors that we are preparing for some kind of military action. Or that some kind of armed conflict has already occurred. The British representatives to the boundary talks, under Governor Douglas's instructions, have taken a more…difficult position."

"Don't you worry," said Harney. "We're going to make Governor Douglas back down in a hurry."

"What are you suggesting, General?" asked Campbell.

In the most patronizing tone possible, Harney said, "Just a little saber rattling, Mister Campbell. A little show of strength to let him know he can't intimidate us."

Campbell, clearly far outside his comfort zone, faced Harney squarely and said, "General Harney, as head of our country's diplomatic mission to the boundary negotiations I must formally ask that you not interfere in this matter."

"You just handle the diplomatic end, Mister Campbell, and don't try to interfere in military matters."

"But it's precsely that kind of talk that's making it so difficult to handle the diplomatic end, as you put it."

Harney turned away from Campbell and told Casey, "I've sent your troop ship up to Whatcom to take Captain Pickett's company out to San Juan Island."

Campbell blurted, "But that's a direct violation of…"

"That'll be all, Mister Campbell," said Harney.

Casey said, "Once again, General, I must protest that I was not consulted about an order given to an officer serving under my command."

Harney continued, "I'll make my headquarters at Fort Townsend for the duration of the San Juan campaign. If Captain Pickett needs anything from you, he'll let you know."

"As I understand it, then," said Casey, "I am to stand by and await orders from one of my subordinates."

"Any communication from Captain Pickett may be taken as coming from my authority."

Harney walked out of the office.

Campbell said, "Colonel, I'm afraid the British will consider this a flagrant violation of trust."

"They ought to," sighed Casey. "It is. Would you ask my orderly to step in for a moment?"

Campbell left the office. Casey sat down, took a sheet of paper from a desk drawer, and reached for his pen and his ink bottle.

Campbell and the orderly returned.

To Campbell, Casey said, "This is an urgent communication to General Scott, Commanding General of the Army in Washington, DC."

To the orderly, he said, "Send it by special messenger to Fort Vancouver with instructions to send it up the Columbia to The Dalles and then overland at all possible speed."

To Campbell again, he said, "I suggest you take whatever measures you can think of to keep the lid on this thing. I'm sorry to say that this is all I'm able to do."

Casey began to write as the orderly escorted Campbell out of the office.

In the waterfront village on San Juan Island, Higgins stood behind the counter of his new store. He flicked a speck of dust off the counter as he admired the well-stocked shelves around the walls and the displays of hardware and dry goods in the middle of the room. Then he turned and slightly repositioned a few objects on the shelves behind him.

His wife surveyed the inventory with a critical eye.

"You should have ordered at least three bolts of the calico," she said. "I can only hope you stocked enough flour and sugar to last until autumn. And why you ordered so many bottles and jugs is beyond me."

The sound of a footstep on the porch drew their attention to the door as Cutler entered.

Higgins immediately became the jovial proprietor, exclaiming, "Well, well, well. Our first customer. Mister Cutler, meet my wife."

"Pleased to meet you," said Cutler.

"Thank you," said Minerva. "How can we help you?"

With a nervous glance at Minerva, Cutler said to Higgins, "Well, now, I've been a sodbuster and a prospector and one thing and another. Never been one to go out of my way to impress anybody."

Higgins, groping for an appropriate response, said, "They say the simple virtues are the best."

As politely as he could, Cutler turned away from Minerva and lowered his voice as he said to Higgins, "A good old bar of soap's always been good enough for me. But now I'm wondering if maybe…well, you know…for the sake of…well, when a man meets a lady that he thinks is pretty special…"

"Lilac water," said Higgins.

"Huh?"

"You want lilac water."

"I do?"

Higgins took a bottle from the shelf and placed it on the counter in front of Cutler.

"When you want to make an especially good impression, splash some of this wherever you think it will do the most good."

Cutler picked up the bottle, uncorked it, took a cautious sniff, and said, "Kind of a sissy smell, isn't it?"

"The ladies are partial to men who use it," Higgins replied.

"Okay, then, I'll take it."

A sandy beach with madrona trees, blackberry bushes, and small evergreens on the higher ground behind the driftwood logs which had been storm-tossed well above the normal high tide level made an attractive destination for an afternoon walk. Cutler and Marlene reached that destination, stepping through an opening in the underbrush and hesitating at the edge of the eighteen-inch drop to the beach. Cutler stepped across the gap onto a log and was turning to assist Marlene when she stepped nimbly onto it beside him. He jumped down to the sand and turned around again; this time, with a sly smile, she extended a hand and allowed Cutler to assist her in stepping down.

This, as they had both anticipated, made it inevitable that she would lean gently against him as she said, "Thank you."

Striking a pose of overdone gallantry, he replied, "My pleasure."

Still holding her hand, he led her out onto the beach, saying, "I've been wanting to get a chance to explain some things. About that pig, I mean, and my spuds. You see, I've been counting on the money from the spuds to…"

"I know. To get down to Frisco, as you call it. Miss Griffin and I were there for a week before we came on up here. I'm sure you'd have a good time there."

"That was my first thought. But then I got to thinking:

there's other things a man can do with a little grubstake."

He gave her a look that clearly indicated the nature of the attraction that might outweigh the attractions of Frisco.

"So when that pig got in my spuds again, and there you were, laughing at me, and me making a fool of myself…"

"I'm afraid I caused you to get yourself in a lot of trouble."

"Oh, it'll blow over. Fainworthy's warrant isn't worth much without Sam's backing. And our whole plan is for Sam and Ike to take it real slow until things simmer down."

They walked in silence down to the water's edge. Then Cutler said, "Do you like working for Miss Griffin?"

"It has its points. I will say the traveling around's been some fun."

"Ever thought of settling down?"

"Now exactly what do you mean by that?"

"Well, I mean have you ever thought of getting married?"

"I guess I'll think about that when the right man asks me."

They were silent for a long moment. Cutler appeared to be bracing himself to ask the question that a man might be expected to ask after such a statement. Then he slowly released the deep breath he had taken and said, "Nice of Miss Griffin to give you the afternoon off."

Marlene's air of expectation subsided, and she said, "It's only because his nibs is calling on her again."

"Fainworthy?"

Marlene nodded.

Cutler went on: "Sometimes I think he's got his sights set on her, and other times I wonder."

"Oh, I've no patience with him, and no more does she. It's always *Permit me to say* and *Your devoted servant.*"

"The cultured approach," said Cutler.

"There's some as might wonder if it was *any* kind of an approach. Not but what a lady has a right to expect a gentleman to be polite. But he's no right to leave her wondering about his intentions."

"A man should make his intentions clear, you think?"

"It's only right."

Cutler took her in his arms with her willing approval.

"Permit me to say," said Cutler, "that I intend to kiss you."

"Your devoted servant might say that you're taking your sweet time getting around to it."

As they kissed, Fainworthy and Mary stepped out of the underbrush and down to the beach a short distance away.

"Potts!" Mary exclaimed as Fainworthy said, "I say!"

Cutler, still embracing Marlene, said, "Howdy."

Marlene edged slightly away from Cutler as Fainworthy escorted Mary toward them. Fainworthy said, "Permit me to say, Mister Cutler, that this is rather a public place for… er… that sort of thing."

"It wasn't a minute ago," said Cutler.

Marlene smoothed her dress and patted her hair.

"Oh, by the way, Fainworthy," Cutler added, "it's too bad about your warrant not working out. But I'm sure you'll find it's nicer to settle things in a friendly way."

"I don't believe Sir James is prepared to regard the matter as closed."

With an envious look at Marlene, Mary said, "Mister Fainworthy, perhaps we should walk up to the meadow."

"Of course," he agreed.

They walked back to the log line, where he extended an arm and said, "Permit me."

Mary rested a hand on his arm as she stepped onto a log and then across the narrow gap to the ground above the beach.

Cutler grinned and said to Marlene, "Your obedient servant" before kissing her again.

~ 15 ~

Fort Bellingham stood on a bluff overlooking the water, which was the only open space near the bay. It had been built three years earlier to protect the settlers of Bellingham Bay, the San Juans, Whidbey Island, and Port Townsend from attacks by northern Indians.

The Army had acquired the property from its owners, who had declined to sell, by the simple expedient of removing the roof of their house while the husband was away, thus forcing his many-months-pregnant wife to walk the three and a half miles into Whatcom in search of other lodgings.

The eighty-foot square fort was enclosed by a pallisade with blockhouses at two opposite corners. Among the features of the area outside the wall was a large garden.

The drudgery of manual labor and the seemingly endless work in the garden outside contributed to the rate of desertion, drunkenness, and lack of respect for military manners that accounted for the high occupancy rate of the fort's jail.

The soldiers under Captain Pickett's command could probably have hit the side of a barn from a reasonable distance away (one visiting officer had suggested that being inside the barn might increase their chances); but, in a test conducted according to Army standards, only one out of forty could hit an ordinary target at a distance of two hundred yards.

On this particular summer day, soldiers inside the fort were polishing three small artillery pieces when a courier rode in through the main gate, dismounted in front of the company office, hitched his horse to the rail, and went inside.

A moment later Captain Pickett, carrying a document, came out followed by the courier.

"Corporal!" Pickett called.

One of the soldiers polishing the artillery pieces hurried to the office and stood at attention.

"Sound Assembly," Pickett ordered.

"Yes, sir," replied the corporal. He stepped up onto the porch, took down a bugle that was hanging near the office door, and stepped back out onto the parade ground. He paused a moment, buzzing his lips and then blowing silently through the bugle; then he raised it and sounded the call for Assembly.

Soldiers came running in through another gate

holding hoes, rakes, and shovels at port arms. As each soldier reached the parade ground, he placed his implement on a long rack and ran to another rack where he grabbed his rifle and fell into formation facing the company office.

Pickett stepped down from the front porch of the office building and walked out to address the troops.

"On orders from General Harney, this company will immediately take possession of San Juan Island. Full field packs. Full armament. March formation in thirty minutes. Dismissed!"

The soldiers dispersed to prepare for their mission.

At the Whatcom waterfront, Pickett's troops stood in formation as hostlers led mules pulling the three artillery pieces out onto the pier and across a wide ramp onto the waiting American vessel. Loungers, drifters, longshoremen, teamsters, crewmen from various ships, and townspeople helped by watching.

Pickett stood at the head of the pier watching the operation until he was approached by Miss La Belle and Nicole, Martine, and Giselle.

"How very exciting, Captain Pickett. Where are they going?"

"I'm afraid I'm not at liberty to divulge that information, Miss La Belle."

A newsboy walked among the spectators with an armload of single-sheet editions, holding one high in the air.

"Extra!" he called. "*Whatcom Chronicle* special edition! Fort Bellingham troops take possession of San Juan Island!"

People clustered around the newsboy, who did a brisk business exchanging papers for coins. Then he moved on, shouting, "*Whatcom Chronicle* extra! Showdown with British Columbia! United States prepares for war with England!"

As the newsboy made a dozen more sales, Miss La Belle said to Pickett, "It looks like the information has already been divulged, Captain."

At a command from the sergeant, the troops straggled onto the pier toward the waiting ship. At the same time, Archibald Campbell hurried down the street to the pier and reached Pickett as Miss La Belle and her girls moved along.

"Excuse me," he gasped. "May I have a word with you, Captain Pickett?"

"At your service," Pickett replied. "How are you, Mister Campbell?"

"I'm extremely concerned, sir. I wonder if we might have a few moments to discuss this matter."

"I'm afraid I'm not at liberty to discuss military matters with a civilian."

"But, Captain, what you're doing will seriously undermine the progress we've made toward a peaceful settlement of the boundary issue."

"As to that, sir," said Pickett, "I can only say that I must obey my orders."

"But what exactly are your orders? Surely, as our country's chief negotiator, I should be kept informed of developments. It might even be thought that I should have had a voice in deciding…"

"I'm sorry, Mister Campbell. If you'll excuse me."

As Pickett followed his troops onto the pier, Campbell pushed through the crowd of bystanders until he found the newsboy and bought a paper which he scanned in dismay.

On a nearby beach, two drifters helped a hooch merchant named Withers load cases of booze and a rolled-up tent into a small catboat which was half afloat on the incoming tide. Then Withers climbed into the boat, and the drifters shoved it free of the beach before sprawling over the gunwales and dragging themselves aboard. Withers unshipped his oars, turned the boat, and rowed further out before signalling his companions to unfurl and raise the sail.

At the pier where Pickett's men were boarding their ship, journalists and gamblers boarded the *Sylvia*.

On the other side of the pier, another hooch merchant named Murphy took the helm of a small sloop as Muldoon, his brawny assistant, shoved it away and vaulted aboard. Muldoon raised and set the jib as Murphy steered the boat into open water. Then Muldoon hoisted the mainsail and the little vessel scooted away.

Late in the afternoon, Fainworthy and Mary stood near the pier below Bellevue Farm where the *Beaver* waited with steam up and deckhands ready to cast off the mooring lines.

Fainworthy said, "I have spoken with your uncle, and he gives his approval to your coming to Victoria for the week of the concerts. Of course you will stay with Sir James and Lady Douglas."

"I look forward to it very much."

As they gazed at each other somewhat more ardently than on any previous occasion, their attention was diverted by the sight of Pickett's troop ship steaming into the bay. They watched with only moderate interest, and Fainworthy said, "One finds so few opportunities to share any type of cultural experience with…may I say a kindred soul?"

"You're too kind, Mister Fainworthy."

"I do wish you'd call me *Percy*."

Mary allowed him to take her hands in his as the ship reversed its engine and glided to a halt. She was about to reply when the splash of the ship's anchor riveted Fainworthy's attention. He dropped her hands and exclaimed, "I say! That's a Yankee troop ship!"

Soldiers on deck watched as a boat was lowered and a rope ladder unfurled over the side of the ship. Four oarsmen climbed down the rope ladder and took up their positions in the boat. Then Pickett climbed down, and when he was seated the oarsmen pulled for the beach.

As two of the oarsmen climbed out into knee-deep water and pulled the bow well up onto the gravel, Fainworthy took a few steps in their direction. As Pickett moved forward and stepped ashore, Mary came to Fainworthy's side and held his arm. Pickett approached, bowed to Mary, and said to Fainworthy: "Captain Pickett, sir. Company D, Ninth Infantry."

Fainworthy executed his minimalist nod, saying, "Percival Fainworthy. Chief aide to Governor Sir James Douglas."

"Please convey my compliments to Governor Douglas at your earliest convenience. And may I be presented to the lady?"

"Miss Griffin. The niece of Mister Griffin, who is in charge of Bellevue Farm on this island."

"Charmed, Miss Griffin," said Pickett.

"Thank you, Captain," she replied.

Fainworthy said, "As the...may I say...ranking representative of Her Majesty's government currently on this island, I must ask to know the reason for your presence here."

"I am about to land my company and establish a military post."

Fainworthy, aghast at encountering arrogance comparable to his own, said, "When I speak with Sir James later this evening, what reason shall I give him for this invasion of British soil?"

"Not an invasion, Mister Fainworthy. Merely a peaceful occupation of American soil to safeguard the interests of American citizens."

"From what danger, may I ask?"

"From possible interference with their liberty."

To Mary, Fainworthy said, "Miss Griffin...Mary...my duty requires me to sail immediatley for Victoria."

"Of course, Mister Fainworthy. Percy."

Pickett said, " Will you be remaining on the island, Miss Griffin?"

"Yes. I'm spending the summer at Bellevue Farm."

"Then with your permission...and yours, Mister Fainworthy...may I escort you home? Then I will have to proceed with the landing of my men."

Fainworthy nodded without speaking, then turned and strode to the pier and out to the *Beaver*.

Pickett and Mary walked up the path to Bellevue Farm.

Shortly after the *Beaver* steamed away, the *Sylvia* came around the wooded headland and drifted up to the pier. The local women and children who customarily met the boat backed away as gamblers, journalists, and curiosity seekers came ashore.

Campbell broke free of the crowd and looked around, finally crossing toward the store as being the most authoritative-looking structure in the waterfront community. Higgins stood on the porch watching all the activity.

At Campbell's approach, Higgins descended the step and asked, "Is it war?"

"I don't know," Campbell admitted. "Is there a government representative on the island?"

"Which government?" Higgins asked.

"American."

Higgins nodded toward Pickett, who was returning from Bellevue Farm, and said, "I guess he's in charge now."

By nightfall, Withers and his two helpers had beached their catboat between the pier and the headland and had erected their tent near Higgins's store. Murphy and Muldoon had tied their sloop to the pier and had set up their tent near the convergence of the two paths(or, to acknowledge the new conditions, the path and the road) coming down to the waterfront. Both tents were doing a lively trade in alcoholic spirits of dubious origin.

Other newcomers were setting up tents or sitting

around campfires, many of them continuing to enjoy the purchases they had made from Withers or Murphy.

A few soldiers were among the players in the half-dozen card games being hosted by recent arrivals whose eagerness to make new friends paired nicely with their uncanny knack of drawing more aces than the other fellow.

The troop ship was anchored out in the bay, and the beach at the foot of the bluff was now the temporary resting place of a dozen small craft.

On the open ground above the bluff across the path from Bellevue Farm, Company D's three field pieces were lined up ten yards apart facing the water. The soldiers had set up rows of small tents back near the bushes and, near the settlers' flagpole, a larger tent that served as company headquarters. In front of the HQ tent, a hastily-painted sign on a piece of board nailed to a tall post read *Camp Pickett.*

~ 17 ~

The next morning, the Victoria waterfront on Vancouver Island was nearly as busy as the waterfront at the little town of Whatcom. Naval and merchant vessels were tied up at the wharf, and others were anchored in the harbor. Across the street that paralleled the waterfront were taverns, lodgings, and small shops. A short distance up the wide street leading into the center of town were government office buildings.

Sailors of the Royal Navy hurried through the streets to report to their ships. Wives and sweethearts clung to many of them and then stood back with the other observers to wave and call encouragement.

Provisioners delivered supplies to the warships, where officers supervised everything.

A newsboy circulated through the crowd calling, "Yankees mobilize! Royal Navy prepares for battle! Will it be war?"

Squads of marines marched down the main street and dispersed to waiting ships.

Captain Hornby, the young officer temporarily in command of the naval fleet in British Columbia, walked down the gangplank of *HMS Tribune* and worked his way across the crowded street and up the steps of a government building. At the moment, the only higher authority in the colony was Governor Douglas; and Hornby was deeply concerned about the orders he was carrying out at the Governor's direction.

In the Governor's office, Sir James Douglas stood at a window observing the activity half a block away. At Hornby's entrance, he turned and scowled.

"Is there a problem, Captain Hornby?" he asked. "It would appear that everything is proceeding satisfactorily."

"I thought, considering the nature of my orders, it would be as well to confirm them personally."

Sir James said, "Your orders are to take possession of San Juan Island."

Hornby took a deep breath before replying, "I hoped… that is, I thought there might have been some…misunderstanding."

"Did I fail to express myself clearly?"

"Not at all, Sir James. But considering the progress of the boundary talks, and knowing that Admiral Baynes would be extremely reluctant to jeopardize that progress…"

"In the temporary absence of Admiral Baynes, I exercise his full authority."

Hornby hastened to say, "Of course. I only wanted to be certain of my orders."

"Take possession of San Juan Island. When you have done so, arrest a man named Lyman Cutler. At the point of a bayonet if necessary. Send him here under armed guard to stand trial in a British court. Those are your orders."

"And if the Americans should offer armed resistance?"

"I am sending you wth three warships and eight hundred marines. I trust that this force will be sufficient to take and hold the ground."

"Very good, Sir James."

Hornby bowed and left the office.

~ 18 ~

Minerva Higgins came out of the store, ostensibly to sweep the front porch. Normally, she would have delegated this part of the morning routine to her hsuband; but now it gave her an opportunity to survey the results of the previous night's activities. She stood with her broom poised and swept a critical gaze across the landscape before her: tents, campsites, and two incredibly delapidated-looking shanties had already been added to the little community now known as San Juan Town.

A soldier lay passed out on the ground in front of the store with his head resting, if it could be called *resting*, on the step. Loud, irregular snoring drew Minerva's attention to a drifter and another soldier slumbering nearby.

"Norbert!" she shouted.

Higgins rushed out the door. Minerva pointed the broom toward the soldier at the foot of the step and then toward the other soldier and the drifter nearby. Higgins looked at them in disgust.

"Well?" she said.

"Well, what?" my dear.

Other soldiers, drifters, journalists, gamblers, and interested parties began to stagger out of tents and to crawl out from behind bushes.

Higgins explained to his wife, "I don't know what we can do."

Minerva stormed down the step and thumped the soldier on the ribs with her broom. He moaned, stirred, and rolled over. She thumped him on the back and then stepped quickly away as he staggered to his feet.

Minerva turned and applied the same treatment to the drifter and the other soldier, who responded in similar fashion. As the drifter focused his eyes on his assailant, he took a belligerent step toward her and reached out to grab her broom. She raised it high overhead and whacked him on the top of the head, sending him to his knees. He staggered to his feet, turned on her again, saw the look in her eyes as she raised the broom for another application of the treatment, and staggered away in the opposite direction.

From Camp Pickett came the sound of the bugler blowing Reveille. The dozen or more soldiers in San Juan Town trudged up the path to report for duty.

McGregor came down the road to the store and exchanged greetings with Higgins and his wife.

"How's business?" he asked.

Higgins answered, "There isn't any."

"Nobody wanting to buy hardware and dry goods, eh?"

Minerva said, "It seems they're only interested in wet goods."

Higgins asked, "And how's the lumber business?"

"Dead. That bloody Fainworthy shut me down. I tell ye, the man needs to be sorted out. But never mind him. I'm here to put some business in your way."

"Well, step right in," said Higgins, holding the door open.

"Now," Higgins continued as he closed the door behind McGregor and Minerva, "what can I get for you?"

"Jugs. Or bottles. Whatever you've got."

Minerva directed his attention to shelves of glassware, crockery, and canning supplies.

"How many will you need?" asked Higgins.

McGregor replied, "All of 'em. And corks."

As Higgins took two jugs off the shelf and put them on the counter, his wife asked McGregor, "What on earth are you planning to do with them all?"

McGregor replied, "There's other things can be done with a steam plant than running a saw."

"You mean a still?" Higgins asked, placing two more jugs on the counter.

"Aye. I've saved the boiler and some other things and got a coil of brass tubing, no matter where, and I've set 'em up where that bloody Englishman won't find 'em. It's like your missuz said: it's wet goods these people want."

Minerva said, "Do I understand that you intend to manufacture liquor and put it in these containers?"

"Aye."

As Higgins put two more jugs on the counter, Minerva stepped between the counter and McGregor and said, "Mister Higgins and I will not be parties to such an enterprise."

Higgins said, "We won't?"

McGregor said, "All ye're bein' a party to is sellin' some jugs."

"Absolutely not. We will not encourage the use of Demon Rum."

"Whisky. Not rum."

"It's all the same," declared Minerva.

"Not to the man that drinks it," muttered McGregor.

Higgins sadly returned the jugs to the shelf as McGregor left the store.

Cutler walked down the path from his cabin and paused to observe the activity at Camp Pickett, where soldiers were digging a trench and piling up the dirt to form a defensive earthwork. From an open window at the farmhouse he heard Mary saying, "Now, Uncle Charles, you know better."

Then Griffin's voice came: "Eh? Oh. Of course, my dear. You're right."

Griffin came out onto the porch, paused to light a cigar,

then walked out to the gate.

"Morning," said Cutler.

"Good morning, my boy."

"I suppose Miss Griffin and Marlene…I mean Miss Potts…are busy packing for their week in Victoria."

"Yes," Griffin said with a contented sigh. "Oh, of course I'll miss her most awfully and all that sort of thing. Fine girl, you know. Can't imagine what I'll do without her around."

"Probably smoke indoors and sit around with your boots off."

Griffin sighed, not so contentedly this time.

"Sometimes I envy you, my boy. Call your soul your own and so forth."

"Well, envy me while you can. You never know when I may hitch up and let a good woman take care of me."

Sam Pike walked up the path from San Juan Town.

Cutler greeted him with, "Howdy, Sam. I thought you went back to Victoria. You here to watch the war?"

"I'm here to arrest you."

Griffin snorted and said, "Is that young poop Fainworthy still trying to make trouble about my pig?"

Sam said, "He's the one that made me a Stipendiary Magistrate."

"I don't even know what that means," Cutler said.

Griffin said, "It means that young blot hasn't got the gumption to come and arrest you himself."

"He tried it once," Cutler reminded Griffin. "But then

he had a squad of marines with him."

Pike said, "And now he's sent me out here alone to do the job. He and that precious Governor of his expect me to take you back to Victoria to stand trial. And from the looks of things over there, they've got something mighty serious cooked up in case I don't bring you in. I'm damned if I can figure out a way to avoid it without putting my own head in a noose and maybe causing a whole lot more trouble in the bargain."

Sutherland, McCleary, and Gorst left Camp Pickett, exchanged greetings with the men at the gate, and started down the path.

Cutler said, "I think I do" and called to the soldiers, "Hang on a minute, would you, fellas?"

The soldiers stopped and turned around, and Cutler continued: "I'd be obliged if you'd put me under arrest."

Griffin said to Pike, "By Jove, that just might work! Jimmy and his trained monkey can't expect you to arrest him if he's already been arrested by the Americans."

Gorst said, "I don't get it."

"You've arrested me. On orders of Captain Pickett. For loitering without a permit, maybe."

Griffin said, "Good show. I'll go and see him right now. Let him in on the scheme and so forth."

Pike put in, "With instructions to make sure he doesn't leave the island."

Cutler said, "Hear that, fellas? Don't let me give you the slip."

"What'll we do?" asked McCleary. "Tie you to the flagpole?"

"I've got a better idea," Cutler told him. "Come on. I'll buy you a drink."

Sutherland said, "Now you're talkin' sense," and the three soldiers followed Cutler down the path to San Juan Town.

The San Juan Town pier was jammed with boats. The *Sylvia* lay off among anchored craft of all sizes and types as a vessel at the pier prepared to cast off. Two dozen rowboats and small sailboats were pulled up on the beach; several were being pushed out into the water as several more arrived in the bay.

Two men carried lumber ashore from a large open boat tied to the pier and added it to the piles beside the frame of a house being built near the bluff on the outskirts of the shanty-and-tent town.

Two farm wives, one English and the other American, came down the hill and cautiously approached Higgins's store. Shouting from an open-front tent where a poker game was in progress caused them to halt; a gunshot from somewhere near the beach caused them to turn and hurry back up the hill.

Higgins came out of the store in time to see the women leave and to see Murphy watching Muldoon eject a journalist from his hooch tent. Muldoon's parting words to the would-be customer were, "No credit. If you can't pay, you can't buy."

Withers came out of his tent and called to Murphy, "How's business?"

"Best I've ever done," Murphy replied.

The *Sylvia* found space at the pier, and Ike Webster came ashore along with an assortment of camp followers.

The local women waiting to collect mail from the *Sylvia* were now escorted by their armed husbands, and no children were to be seen.

Higgins hurried down the step to accost Webster, saying, "Mister Webster! You're a Deputy Sheriff. Can you get these hooch merchants away from my property? They're driving away all my customers."

Webster said, "Well, if they don't have a license to sell spirits, I guess I could shut 'em down."

He crossed to Murphy, who was standing outside his tent, and asked, "Can I see your license?"

"Can I see some proof of your authority?" Murphy replied.

Webster took a paper from his inside coat pocket and showed it to Murphy, who said, "American. But this is British territory, and I'm a British subject. So it looks like you don't have any authority over me at all."

Webster said, "Well, then, can I see your British license?"

"I don't know as it's legal to show a British license to an American agent."

Webster turned to confront Withers and asked, "You got a license?"

"I'm a British citizen, too."

Murphy said softly, "A British *subject*, you say? Fancy that."

Withers said, "Yeah. Subject."

Webster said, "Licensed by the British government?"

"Oh, sure. But it ain't legal for me to show you my license on account of you being an American agent."

Higgins erupted: "This is an outrage! Arrest these men for fraud!"

Webster shook his head and declared, "I'd need to check with higher authority for that. Guess I better go see Captain Pickett."

Webster headed up the path as Sam Pike came down. They talked briefly, then Pike came on down to the store where Higgins clutched his arm.

"Mister Pike! You represent the British law!"

"I'm afraid so."

To Murphy and Withers, Higgins said, "You can show your licenses to this gentleman!"

Murphy said, "As an American citizen on American soil, I'm not answerable to a British agent."

Withers said, "Me, either. As an American subject…"

"Citizen," put in Murphy.

"Citizen," Withers amended, "I don't have any answers for a British agent."

"These men are bald-faced liars!" shouted Higgins.

The settlers who had met the *Sylvia* now returned nervously through the settlement, skirting the confrontation in front of the store, and hurried up the road to disperse to their homes in other parts of the island.

Mary and Marlene came down to the pier accompanied by four farmhands carrying their luggage. The ladies and the farmhands darted apprehensive glances in all directions as they made their way to the pier, where they were met by two of the *Beaver*'s crew members. Their ship was anchored in the bay, and there had been just enough room at the pier to accommodate one of the ship's boats.

The crew members and the farmhands got the luggage stowed in the boat and then assisted Mary and Marlene. Mary needed all of her attention for the task of maintaining her dignity in the potentially less-than-dignified process of climbing down into a large open rowboat and sitting on a plank bench. Marlene, on the other hand, stepped lightly into the boat, laughed when its gentle movement made her lose her balance momentarily, and sat happily beside Mary for the short voyage out to the *Beaver*.

President Buchanan sat at his desk reading a brief report. Across from him sat General Winfield Scott, a weathered old soldier with a thick head of white hair and an alert gleam in his eyes.

Buchanan said, "Is it possible that General Harney is actually preparing to go to war over a pig?"

General Scott replied, "Quite possible, in my opinion."

Buchanan said, "I hesitate to request that you go out there yourself. The Commanding General of the Army and a man of your…"

"Age," said Scott to complete the sentence. "But it appears to be necessary. My main concern is that he may be as uncooperative as he was the last time I tried to relieve him of his command."

"This time his friends in Congress will be three thousand miles away. And you will have full written authority to take whatever steps are necessary to restore our friendly relations with the British."

"And if war has already broken out when I arrive?" Scott inquired.

"Then," said the President, "you will take command of our forces and win the war."

On San Juan Island, Captain Pickett stood near the edge of the bluff looking out over the bay, where *HMS Tribune* and two other warships were anchored with their guns run out and their decks packed with marines.

As Pickett watched, Captain Hornby climbed down into a gig and the oarsmen pulled for the beach.

In San Juan Town, Cutler dunked McCleary's face in a bucket of water and then quickly pulled his head back up. McCleary started to gag.

"No more of that," Cutler warned him, and he dunked McCleary's face in the bucket again.

Sutherland and Gorst shook their sopping hair and tried to wipe their faces on their sleeves as Cutler helped McCleary to his feet.

As the soldiers fumbled with their buttons, Cutler sheepdogged them over to a campfire where two drifters, Finley and Creech, were making coffee. Finley leaned over a battered pot suspended over the fire and savored the aroma with epicurean satisfaction while Creech set out two tin cups on a board laid across two rocks as if he were setting a fine table.

"Morning, fellas," said Cutler.

Finley said, "Good morning, sir. But not so good for your friends, eh?"

Cutler said, "I think they could use a cup of that coffee if you could spare it."

Creech said, "Always happy to do a favor for the lads who proudly wear the uniform."

Gorst continued to fumble with the buttons of his tunic, then gave up trying to make both sides of the garment line up properly.

With nudges from Cutler, the three soldiers slouched a few steps closer to the makeshift table as Finley unhooked the pot and poured a cupful.

Creech handed the cup to Cutler, who held it while McCleary slurped at it. Then McCleary took the cup and held it for Sutherland, who took a drink and then reached for the cup and held it for Gorst. Finally Cutler repossessed the cup and handed it back to Creech.

"Much obliged," he said. To the soldiers: "Okay, boys, you better march me out of here."

Pickett passed along the edge of the settlement heading toward the beach as Cutler nudged the soldiers into position for marching him out of there.

By the time Hornby landed at the beach, Pickett stood ready to greet him.

"Captain Pickett, sir," he announced. "United States

Army. How may I have the honor of serving you?"

"Captain Hornby. Her Brittanic Majesty's Royal Navy. Your servant, sir. Perhaps I may save you some...embarrassment."

"Embarrassment, sir?" inquired Pickett.

"I have the honor to inform you, Captain, that you have set up camp on British soil. My officers and men will count it a privilege to assist you in relocating to the U.S. mainland."

Pickett replied, "As my position is already established on American soil, Captain, I must regretfully decline your most generous offer."

"Perhaps, Captain, it would be prudent for you to choose some other location in the interest of avoiding any ill will between our governments."

Pickett's tone and manner became even more dignified and honorable as he said, "I could hardly entertain the suggestion that I abandon my position without an order from the government that sent me here."

Hornby said, "It pains me to state that I, too, have orders to occupy this island. And may I point out, Captain, that I have eight hunderd marines and, I think, a cannon for every man in your company."

Cutler arrived at this moment followed by his unarmed and disheveled escort.

"Sorry to interrupt like this, gents. I'm Lyman Cutler." To Pickett he said, "Your men have arrested me. On your orders."

"Of course," Pickett replied. "Pleased to meet you, Mister Cutler."

Hornby asked, "Is this the man who shot the pig?"

"That's me," Cutler answered.

"Then I suppose," Hornby continued, "that I owe you thanks for being the instrument by which I have had the honor to become acquainted with Captain Pickett."

Cutler shrugged and said, "Well, I sure never meant to cause this big a stir."

Pickett asked, "Is there anything I can do for you, Mister Cutler?"

"Well, I just thought...I mean these soldiers thought maybe they should take me up to your camp."

"Just what I was about to suggest," said Pickett.

Cutler helped the hung-over soldiers turn around and regroup. Then he led them back to the path leading up onto the bluff.

Hornby said, "May I take it, then, that you definitely decline to remove your forces?"

"My orders and my honor leave me no choice but to stand my ground, sir."

"Off the record, Captain Pickett, permit me to say that my own orders to remove you are worded in the most emphatic manner. And if it comes to a clash of arms, there can be no doubt of my victory."

"As to that, sir," replied Pickett, "I will defend my nation's honor and sovereignty to the last man."

Hornby bowed slightly and said, "Then I have the honor to wish you good day, sir."

Pickett, returning the bow, said, "Your most humble servant, sir."

Two oarsmen stood by to steady the gig as Hornby climbed in. Then they pushed it away and scrambled aboard.

Pickett turned away and walked back through San Juan Town.

~ 20 ~

In San Juan Town, the intensity and duration of a night's revelry were not dependent on the hours of sunrise and sunset. It was, as the chronclers of the Old West sometimes put it, a "wide open" town. Well before the end of the summer evening, the brief daytime lull was giving way to renewed activity.

In one of the large hooch tents, Murphy sold liquor by the bottle to a steady stream of customers. Finley and Creech entered as Joe, the farmhand and butler-in-training, paid for a bottle and stepped aside to extract the cork.

Murphy asked, "What'll you have, gentlemen?"

"Two glasses of your finest whisky," Finley answered.

"Bottle sales only," Murphy said.

Creech surveyed the tent with disappointment. Muldoon stood near a stack of crates, and beside Murphy was a battered table holding bottles of liquor and a tin cashbox.

"No bar," Creech observed. "Doesn't seem quite civilized."

Finley agreed: "Where is the atmosphere...the camaraderie...without the polished oak and the brass rail?"

Joe took a long drink from his bottle, then held it up in disgust.

"This whisky's been watered!"

Murphy cautioned him: "Be careful what you accuse people of, my friend."

"I'm accusin' you of waterin' this booze!"

"A discriminating palate," Finley said to Creech.

"A connoisseur, no doubt," Creech replied.

"Gimme my money back!" Joe demanded.

Murphy said calmly, "No refunds."

"You low-down son of a..."

Murphy, still calm, said, "Muldoon, will you show this gentleman out?"

Muldoon hauled Joe to the door and shoved him out.

As Joe stumbled out of the tent, he nearly collided with Griffin, who stepped back and said, "Really, my dear fellow, you ought to be more careful."

Joe glared at Griffin, then shared the glare with a wider world as he stormed away among the tents and shanties.

Griffin continued past the open side of a crowded lean-to where a professional gambler played cards with some of the settlers, including Zeke and Tubby.

"How many more o' them aces have you got up your sleeve?" demanded Zeke.

"You accusing me of cheating?" challenged the

gambler.

"Damn right I am!"

"Nobody calls me a cheater," proclaimed the gambler, pulling a pistol from an unseen shoulder holster.

"I just did!" shouted Zeke, jumping to his feet, upending the card table and knocking the pistol out of the gambler's hand.

Zeke and the gambler brawled and stumbled into Griffin's path. Griffin quickly turned aside between other tents and shanties, where Martine and Giselle accosted him.

"Hello, handsome," said Martine.

"Oh. Ah. Er, good evening...ladies."

"Looking for a couple of naughty girls?" asked Giselle.

"Looking for a couple of naughty boys, actually," Griffin replied.

As Martine and Giselle raised their eyebrows and smiled, Griffin hastily added, "Came down to get the mail hours ago, don't you know, and haven't come back. Seem to think a farm runs itself, by gad."

Martine said, "They're probably having a good time. How about you, honey?"

"Er...thanks awfully, you know...but I really must... er...got to dash along and so forth."

Griffin escaped to the path leading back up to his farm.

~ 21 ~

Sir James, sitting at his desk, watched without enthusiasm as Captain Hornby was shown into his office.

"I'm surprised to see you back here, Captain. I congratulate you on taking the island so promptly."

When Hornby failed to reply immediately, Sir James asked, "You *have* taken possession of the island?"

"In a sense I have, Sir James."

"Then the Yankees have been removed."

"No. But I outnumber them by more than twelve to one, and I have sixty cannons to their three field pieces."

"Are you waiting for reinforcements?"

"Of course not, Sir James."

"Then I fail to understand why you have not carried out my orders."

Hornby explained: "Since we have the ability to occupy the island at any time, I consider our present position virtually tantamount to holding the ground." Hornby swallowed nervously and went on: "In seeking to avoid a clash of arms, as I know Admiral Baynes would wish me to do…"

"I will remind you, Captain, that Admiral Baynes is at sea and that in his absence you are under my orders."

"I understand," said Hornby. "And I have tried to fulfill the intent of those orders without initiating any action that might disrupt the peaceful progress of the boundary negotiations."

"The boundary negotiations are hampering you in the execution of your orders?"

"Permit me to say that the situation is rather complex."

"I appreciate your difficulty, Captain Hornby." Sir James sat down at his desk. "I will do what I can to simplify the situation. Return to your post and be prepared to carry out your orders."

Hornby failed to entirely suppress his concern as he said, "Very good, Sir James."

As Hornby left the office, Sir James reached for paper and pen.

In a Victoria newspaper office, a reporter accepted money from the editor and said, "Front page again, I presume."

"Do you think it's that big a story?" asked the editor.

"Sure. It's a war, after all."

"So far," the editor reminded him, "the only casualty is a pig."

"And so far," said the reporter, "every newsboy on the street has sold every copy he's been given. I tell you the public is hungry for news about this war."

"Well, it's an odd kind of war."

"Everything out here is odd," the reporter said. "The Customs people estimate that only three percent of the British Columbia population is British."

"That's about right, I suppose," said the editor.

"Most of the other ninety-seven percent's Yankees, and there's talk of a revolt. The Governor better watch his step or England'll be losing another colony. Well, I've got to go buy some sailors a drink. I heard that another ship's going over to San Juan."

The reporter cheerfully pocketed his money and left the office.

On the bluff overlooking San Juan Town, Pickett stood observing the scene below. He turned to greet a delegation of American and English settlers led by Webster, Pike, and another newcomer to the island.

"To what do I owe the honor?" Pickett asked.

Webster said, "Me and Sam would like you to meet Judge Crosbie from Seattle."

"A pleasure, Judge," said Pickett. "What brings you to this out-of-the-way spot?"

"Had to hold an inquest on a dead man found over on Lopez Island. Thought I'd drop by here and see what all the fuss is about. These good people" (he indicated the settlers) "thought you and I might work together to help solve some problems you're having."

Pickett looked at Pike and asked Crosbie, "What role did you have in mind for the British representative?"

Webster said, "We thought Sam ought to be involved so as to close a loophole for certain illegal hooch merchants that keep forgetting what country they're a citizen of."

"And also," said Pike, "to assure the authorities in Victoria that nobody's tryin' to slip one over on 'em."

Crosbie said, "And, further, to reassure the English settlers on the island as well as the Americans. Meaning no offense, Captain Pickett, but there seems to be some doubt as to the extent of your enforceable authority."

"I fail to understand you, sir. I am in command of this island."

Two drunk soldiers staggered into camp as gunshots sounded from the town below. Two men ran along the beach, shoved a rowboat into the water, and frantically pulled away. They barely avoided being run down by two more British warships entering the bay.

Pickett said, "I suppose it wouldn't hurt for you to firm up our authority over the civilian population."

"Thank you, Captain. We'll prepare some warrants right away and hold court tomorrow."

On the pier at Whatcom, a newsboy peddled his

papers, accosting passengers arriving from San Francisco with shouts of "Latest from the Pig War!" and "Fort Bellingham troops defend San Juan Island!"

Out on the street, another newsboy greeted arrivals with shouts of "Last chance for Fraser gold rush!" and "English may close border in retaliation for San Juan pig!"

~22~

In a conference room in the Whatcom courthouse, an American flag was displayed on one wall and a British flag on the opposite wall. Easels holding maps stood at each end of a long table. On one side of the table, Campbell sat with two associates. On the other side, the British delegate and his three aides sat stiffly, hardly looking at their counterparts across the table.

The British delegate opened the session by asking Campbell, "Is it true that your Army has taken possession of San Juan Island?"

"I'm afraid so," Campbell admitted.

The British delegate continued: "In order to prevent the lawful arrest and trial of a trespasser who shot another man's pig?"

"Certainly not!" Campbell objected. "The purpose of the occupation is merely to assure the safety of American citizens."

"Did your President or your Congress order this occupation? Because, if so, this must be construed as nothing less than an act of war."

"No...that is...I cannot say that this action represents my government's official policy."

"Do you mean, then, that your military forces have acted without your government's authority?"

"Not precisely that. No. But it would seem that a speedy diplomatic resolution of the boundary issue is our only means of avoiding more aggressive action by either side."

"I will speak more plainly," said the British delegate. "Governor Douglas has instructed me to say that there will be no further talks until your military force has been withdrawn from San Juan Island."

Campbell pleaded, "But that seems far too extreme a position..."

Ignoring the interruption, the British delegate added, "He has further instructed me to inform you that if they are not immediately withdrawn, they will be removed by force of arms."

The British delegate and his aides stood, packed their maps and papers into briefcases, and left the room.

In the middle of San Juan Town, Judge Crosbie sat behind a makeshift table facing a crowd of islanders, gamblers, hooch merchants, camp followers, a few deckhands from merchant vessels, and an assortment of self-styled journalists. Webster and Pike stood beside the table, serving as bailiffs.

Six jurors stood facing Crosbie, who said, "Do you all swear that you are residents in good standing of this place and have been so for a period of at least twelve months prior to the convening of this court?"

The jurors all responded in the affirmative.

"That's a lie!" shouted Clarence from the crowd. "None of them's been here more than a month!"

A gambler in the crowd spoke up: ""I'll vouch for them, Your Honor!"

Tubby shouted, "*He's* only been here a week!"

Crosbie said, "If anyone can show cause why any of these jurors should be disqualified, now's the time to come forward."

Murphy and Muldoon, Withers and his two tough-looking associates turned to face the crowd. The muttering among the resident islanders ceased abruptly.

Crosbie said, "Then this court will come to order."

The jurors sat down on chairs to one side as Webster motioned for Murphy to come forward.

Crosbie glanced at a paper on the table and said, "Mister Murphy, you're charged with selling liquor without a license. How do you plead?"

"Not guilty, Your Honor."

"First witness," said Crosbie.

Joe came forward, and Crosbie said, "Do you swear to tell the truth, the whole truth, and nothing but the truth?"

"Sure I do."

"Good enough," Crosbie sighed. "Did this man sell you liquor?"

"He sure did. Cheap watered-down whisky, the no-good…"

Crosbie said, "That'll do. Thank you. Next witness."

Higgins came forward, and Crosbie asked, "Do you swear to tell the truth, the whole truth, and nothing but the truth?"

"I do, Your Honor."

"Did you see this man selling liquor?"

"I did, Your Honor."

"Thank you. Next witness."

Webster motioned for Muldoon to come forward.

Crosbie swore him in and asked, "To your knowledge, is it true that Mister Murphy has been selling watered whisky?"

"No, sir, it ain't. Murphy's hooch is as good as you can get without buyin' the real stuff. And his price is as low as you'll find anywhere on the island."

"Thank you," said Crosbie. "Next witness."

Webster stood in front of the table, and Crosbie went through the formula.

"Did you ask Mr. Murphy to show you his license to sell liquor?" Crosbie asked.

"Yes, Your Honor. And he refused."

"Next witness," said Crosbie.

Pike came forward and went through the same routine.

"Did you ask Mister Murphy to show you his license?"

Pike said, "I did, Your Honor, but he wouldn't show it to me."

To the jurors, Crosbie asked, "Do you find the defendant guilty or not guilty of selling liquor without a license?"

"Not guilty, Your Honor," said the hastily selected foreman of the jury.

"What!" said Crosbie.

Cheers and shouts from the camp followers drowned out the groans of dismay from the island residents.

"Next case," said Crosbie.

Pike escorted Withers up to face the table.

Crosbie said, "Mister Withers, you're charged with selling liquor without a license. How do you plead?"

"Not guilty. Sir. Your Honor."

"First witness," called Crosbie. Finley stepped up to the table and was sworn in.

"Did you buy liquor from this man?"

"Yes, Your Honor."

Crosbie motioned Finley away and said, "Next witness."

Creech came forward, and after a quick nod to the formalities Crosbie asked, "Did you buy liquor from him?"

"Yes, Your Honor. On several occasions."

Crosbie motioned Creech away as Pike came forward.

"Did this man show you a license?"

"No, Your Honor," Pike replied.

Webster came forward.

"Did he show you one?" asked Crosbie.

"No, Your Honor."

Once again Crosbie addressed the jury: "Now, gentlemen, I want you to carefully consider the testimony you've just heard. Then decide if the defendant is guilty or…"

"Not guilty," said the foreman.

Crosbie pounded the table with his fist and said, "Remaining cases dismissed!"

More cheers erupted from the riff-raff, followed by another cheer when Murphy shouted, "This way, gents! The first round's on me!"

As the crowd dispersed, Pickett walked into the town. Higgins rushed over to him, saying, "You've got to do something. These ruffians are damaging my property and ruining my business. I demand that you get them off the island!"

Pickett replied, "That's being taken care of by the civil authorities."

Higgins pointed to where Crosbie, Webster, and Pike were boarding the *Sylvia*.

"There go the civil authorities!" he said.

In San Juan Town, Minerva Higgins stood at the doorway of the store observing the aftermath of another riotous night. Several of what had formerly been the island's "decent citizens" were among the bedraggled survivors.

Mary and Marlene left the pier followed by farmhands carrying their luggage from the *Beaver*. Pickett and an armed squad of soldiers stood waiting for them as they stepped ashore.

Mary stopped and demanded, "What is the meaning of this, Captain Pickett? Are we to be taken prisoner?"

"My dear Miss Griffin, not at all. My men are here to escort you home."

At a gesture from Pickett, the soldiers stepped back.

"If you will allow us, ladies," Pickett said.

Mary and Marlene exchanged glances and then proceeded. Two soldiers walked ahead of them, one walked on each side, and two more fell in behind the luggage carriers.

Pickett stood watching a succession of San Juan Town's less savory inhabitants step aside for the procession. Miss La Belle and her girls, approaching from the direction of the mostly completed house near the bluff, paused to watch the parade.

"Morning, boys," Nicole called to the soldiers.

"What's your hurry?" Giselle asked them.

Several soldiers winked and smiled at the girls as they passed among the tents and shanties of the settlement.

Miss La Belle watched Pickett approaching and said, "Good morning, Captain Pickett."

"Miss La Belle. Ladies. So nice to see you again."

Touching the brim of his hat, he shoulder-bowed before continuing with his troops and their guests.

At that moment, a gambler backed out from between two shanties with his hands up, followed by another gambler pointing a pistol at him. Seeing the soldiers, they bolted away in different directions.

The inebriated gentleman who had spooked the team of horses on the Whatcom pier two months earlier, and who appeared to be in the same condition this morning, leered at Mary and Marlene and called to their escort: "Hey, sojer boys! This what yuh draw yer pay for?"

McGregor and Joe chased a thief out from behind a tent as the procession passed by. The thief knocked down a luggage-laden farmhand and skidded to a halt beside Mary.

McGregor advanced on the thief, brandishing a club. Beside him, Joe aimed a pistol.

Some soldiers took prompt aim at McGregor and Joe while others aimed uncertainly at the thief. Mary, Marlene, and the farmhands were in the crossfire zone.

Suddenly the thief dashed away in a new direction. McGregor and Joe shoved past the soldiers to pursue him. The soldiers lowered their rifles, and the procession moved on up the path toward Bellevue Farm.

A twenty-foot double-ended open boat converted from oar power to steam power puffed and clanked through the channels that separated the various islands of the San Juan archipelago. The skipper manned the tiller. His young son tended the fire, feeding in short lengths of driftwood and scrap lumber as needed. The paying passengers, Archibald Campbell and the newspaper reporter from Victoria, took turns manning the plunger-type pump that fed bilge water out through a hose draped over the gunwale at approximately the same rate as it seeped in through the poorly caulked seams of the hull.

Campbell asked his companion, who was manning the pump, "Is this your first visit to the scene of operations?"

"No," the reporter answered. "I was out here a week ago."

"So your information is not up to date."

"Oh, it's up to date all right. I have my sources."

"And may I ask what your sources have told you about the situation?"

The reporter grinned and said, "Buy Friday's paper."

Campbell said, "I really would appreciate knowing as much as possible right now."

"You have a special interest in it? Say, you're not from another paper, are you?"

"No, no. My interest is… well, let's just leave it that I'm very interested."

"I can tell you that a declaration of war may come at any moment."

"Governor Douglas is entirely too impetuous," said Campbell.

"I didn't say Douglas. But that's all I can say at the moment."

Campbell groaned, then said, "Here. Let me pump for a while. That seems to be all I'm good for."

Colonel Casey stood alone in the office at Fort Townsend that General Harney had taken over for the duration of what he called the San Juan campaign. Eventually Casey walked to the window and looked out to observe the activity of the fort.

There was no activity to be observed.

Casey returned to his position in the center of the office and finally heard voices in the hallway. The loudest, not to his surprise, was General Harney's.

"Every last one of them! By tonight!" said Harney to some unseen but no doubt cringing subordinate.

Harney entered the office and stood looking at Casey without speaking. At last Casey said, "Reporting as ordered, General."

"Naturally," Harney growled. "I want you to be ready to reinforce Captain Pickett promptly when… if the shooting starts."

"Begging the General's pardon, but wouldn't it be better to reinforce Captain Pickett now in the hope of discouraging a Britsh attack?"

"Leave the strategy to me, Colonel. You just be ready to get your men out there when Captain Pickett sends the word."

"There seems to be no doubt that San Juan Island will become a battlefield," said Casey.

"We'll see, Colonel," said Harney. "We'll see."

~24~

In San Juan Town's hardware and dry goods store, McGregor was putting jugs and bottles into crates as fast as Higgins removed them from the shelves.

Minerva came in through the door behind the counter. "What do you think you're doing?" she demanded.

"Transacting business," Higgins replied.

"I told this man that we would not do business with him."

"And *I'm* telling *you* that he and I are going into business together."

"How dare you..."

"Minerva," Higgins told her, "be quiet."

"Well, I never!"

McGregor said, "Well, try it once."

Minerva squeaked in astonishment and said, "Norbert! Are you going to let him speak to me that way?"

"Yes," Higgins said. "Wish I'd had the gumption to do it myself a long time ago."

Higgins continued taking jugs and bottles from the shelves. McGregor continued packing them into crates. Minerva continued scowling for a long moment before flouncing out through the door behind the counter.

In the late afternoon, fog came to the San Juan Islands. It rolled in very slowly from Rosario Strait to the east, over the lowest points of Orcas, Shaw, and Lopez Islands; and it drifted up from Admiralty Inlet, engulfing Fort Townsend on its way across Port Townsend and the Strait of Juan de Fuca.

By nightfall, most of the San Juans and the surrounding waters were fogged in.

Cutler walked down the path from his cabin, glancing at vague figures moving among the faint glows of a dozen fires at Camp Pickett. He heard a gasp from near the Bellevue Farm gate before he could see the gate or the dim figure standing on the path in front of it.

"Mister Cutler?" asked Mary's voice.

"Yep," said Cutler, moving close enough for them to see each other. "Sorry to startle you. Were you expecting me?"

"I was waiting for...someone else."

"Oh. Well, I was coming to call on Miss Potts. If you don't mind, that is."

"Certainly. I'm sure she'll be glad to see you as soon as she and my uncle return from the village. But since you're here, I wonder if you could spare a few minutes to...help me with something."

"Sure thing. What is it?"

Mary took a deep breath, let it out, and said, "As you may know, Mister Fainworthy has been...calling on me... occasionally."

"So I've noticed," Cutler said with a grin. "He seems to find plenty of occasions."

"He is coming here this evening. I believe his boat is already in the harbor."

"I hope so, for his sake," Cutler said. "It can't be safe out on the water in fog like this. But in that case you'll want me to take care of whatever it is and be on my way. As you may have noticed, he and I don't exactly take to each other."

"I know. There is a certain...directness about you, Mister Cutler. A sort of...zest. I suppose it comes from living on the frontier."

"Could be. Is that what your Mister Fainworthy dislikes about me?"

"Mister Fainworthy is more..."

"Civilized?"

"Restrained, let us say."

Cutler nodded. "Not much of a firecracker. Except when he's getting up warrants to have other people arrested." His smile, like his nod, was lost on Mary. "But I still don't know what you want me to do for you."

"Mister Fainworthy hesitates to...well, to put it bluntly, it occurred to me that if he found us here together he might..."

"I get it. If he thought somebody else was jumping his claim, he might work it a little harder himself."

"I suppose that does express what I mean."

They heard footsteps in the fog. Mary stepped closer to Cutler and whispered, "Mister Cutler, would you mind... embracing me?"

"Embracing you?"

"Would you please hold me in your arms?"

As the footsteps came closer, Mary threw herself against Cutler. As he wrapped his arms around her, he whispered, "This oughta make him jealous, all right."

Leaning her head back, she whispered, "There's just one more thing."

She raised her face and kissed him. He responded politely, but she quickly entered more thoroughly into the spirit of the thing. Cutler was trying to extricate himself when Griffin and Marlene emerged from the fog.

"By gad, sir!" said Griffin. "Mary, my dear, what the devil is this fellow doing? Well, I mean to say I can see very well what he's doing, dash it! Sir, I never would have taken you for a wrong 'un!"

Marlene said, "And to think I ever..."

"You don't understand," Cutler blurted.

"Oh, don't I?" said Marlene.

Griffin said, "Not the straight bat, by gad! Not the done thing!"

Cutler said, "But we were only…that is, we were expecting Fainworthy…"

Marlene said, "Mister Fainworthy sends his respects and says he'll be delayed for a few more minutes. Not but what that'll be good news for some people."

"But, Marlene."

"My name is Potts. *Miss* Potts."

Griffin said, "If I thought a niece of mine would accept the addresses of one man and then let another man…"

"You've got to let me explain. Miss Griffin and I weren't…I mean, we're just…"

"Engaged," blurted Mary.

Griffin said, "What? You mean, to be married?"

Mary cast an anxious glance at Cutler and said, "Yes."

"Well, dash it, why didn't you say so?" To Marlene: "Go tell that young poop we don't care how long he's delayed. The longer the better. No, wait. Can't have you going back down there alone. Go on into the house and I'll take care of him."

Marlene circled Mary and Cutler in silence, opened the gate in silence, slammed it closed, and vanished into the fog.

Griffin grabbed Cutler's hand and shook it, saying, "Congratulations, my boy. Quite a surprise, I must say. Thought Mary was a bit sweet on that young…"

"Uncle Charles, please!"

"Eh? Oh, certainly, certainly. You two will want to be alone, eh?"

Chuckling, Griffin turned and started back down the path into the fog, only to reappear a moment later saying, "By the way, my dear fellow, you'll have dinner with us tonight, of course. We're having pork roast. I know how partial you are to my pigs."

Griffin, still chuckling, vanished once more into the fog.

Mary stepped away from Cutler and said, "I'm so sorry, Mister Cutler. But it was the only thing I could think of to say. What are we going to do now?"

"I have no idea," Cutler said.

~25~

Among the fog-bound tents and shanties of San Juan Town, business was less brisk than usual. At the hardware and dry goods store, however, the windows gave out enough light to show dim figures climbing the step and entering the building, and the loudest sounds of merriment seemed to come from there.

Inside the store, a transformation had taken place. The main counter had become a saloon bar. The merchandise on the shelves behind the bar now shared space with dozens of bottles, some bearing the labels of known distilleries and others sporting home-made labels which had been produced as quickly and individually as the contents they identified. Prime counter space had been allocated to a beer keg.

The center of the room had been cleared of merchandise to make room for half a dozen poker tables.

Customers entering the store were met by Miss La

Belle, who checked their hats, and by Clarence and Zeke, who checked their guns. Tubby served the throng at the bar. Higgins circulated among the patrons.

Finley and Creech, resting their backs against the bar, surveyed the busy room with approval.

"Still no polished oak," said Finley. "No brass rail. But quite a decent substitute. Now we have some atmosphere… a touch of that *ambience* that makes all the difference."

Creech added, "And the camaraderie. Heart-warming. Really quite heart-warming."

Suddenly two gamblers started to scuffle with shouts of "I saw you palm that queen!" and "How many jacks do you have in this deck?"

Just as suddenly, four farmhands converged on them, pinned their arms, and hustled them to the door. Zeke frisked the gamblers for hat-check tickets which they gave to Miss La Belle, who found the gamblers' hats and plopped them on their heads before the farmhands marched them out the door.

The players at another card table, observing the ejection, looked concerned.

The dealer said, "Excuse me, gentlemen. I'm afraid I've miscounted."

"Oh, dear," said another player. "That's too bad."

"I'll deal again, if you don't mind."

Another player said, "By all means. The only thing to do." As he placed his cards face down to be re-shuffled, he surreptitiously added two aces from up his sleeve.

As another player shoved his cards across the table, he glanced at the floor with overdone nonchalance, leaned over, and came up with a card from under his chair, saying, "Why, look what I found on the floor. The wind must have blown it there."

The dealer gathered up the cards, shuffled them thoroughly, and dealt them again with scrupulous accuracy.

McGregor entered through the door behind the counter and beckoned to Higgins, who went back out with him. Soon they returned with cases of jugs and bottles which they unpacked and set on the shelves.

On the west side of the island, which was fully as fogged in as San Juan Town, a lone oarsman propelled his rowboat toward the beach where Alf, Tom, Will, and Jack had hidden their boat on the day of the rabbit hunt. The figure in the boat climbed out, grabbed a coiled rope which was attached to the bow, and paid it out as he stumbled up the beach to the log line. He tied the rope around the stub of a branch on a driftwood log, climbed over the log, scrambled up into the underbrush and was gone.

At Bellevue Farm, Griffin, Mary, Cutler, and Pickett were at the dinner table. Joe served the various dishes, removed bowls and plates, filled wine glasses, and otherwise performed his new duties in a manner which, although it embarrassed Mary, was entirely acceptable to Griffin and Cutler. Pickett's Southern grace and tact made it impossible to tell whether or not he found any flaws in Joe's performance.

Mary, glancing at the window, said, "The fog seems to be getting thicker, if such a thing were possible."

Griffin said, "We generally get some thick ones this time of year."

"Pretty extreme tides right now, too," said Cutler.

"We get these nasty ones every few months," Griffin said. "Low tides so far out you'd swear you could walk over to Lopez Island without wetting your boots, and highs that either just come in a few feet or else wash right up to the trees."

Pickett said, "I'm informed that we can expect these minus tides for another three days."

"What does that mean?" Mary asked. "What are minus tides?"

Griffin explained: "You see, the tide comes in and goes out twice in every twenty-four hours, or roughly that. Some high tides come in farther than others, and some low tides go out farther than others, if you follow me. But every few months we get some that put the ordinary low tides to shame. Those are minus tides."

Cutler added, "Where you'd normally stand at the water's edge at low tide, at a minus tide you can walk another twenty yards or more to the water. Places where the water's normally six or eight or ten feet deep at low tide are high and dry on a minus tide."

Mary said, "Well, I'm thankful that I'm not out there in this fog standing at the water's edge, however low it may be."

Outside the farmhouse fence, Sutherland, McCleary, and Gorst were on sentry duty. Heavy breathing and rustling of bushes attracted their attention.

Peering into the fog, Gorst shouted, "Hey, who's that? I mean, halt! Who goes there?"

A lone figure stumbled out of the fog and was promptly grabbed by Sutherland and McCleary.

Gorst ran to the front door and knocked, waited a few seconds, then knocked again. Finally Joe opened the door and said, "Good evening, sir or… well, just sir. Please come inside."

Joe stood back and extended the tray, but Gorst stayed on the porch and said, "Just tell Captain Pickett he's needed out here."

Joe started to return to the dining room, then stopped, lowered the empty card tray, turned back toward the front door. Marlene came out of the door at the back of the hallway carrying a loaded dessert tray. Joe looked to her for instruction.

Gorst said, "Of, for the love of… Captain Pickett!"

A moment later Pickett hurried out of the dining room followed by Cutler and Griffin. Mary stopped just outside the dining room as the men continued to the front door. Marlene came a few steps closer to the action but made a point of halting well short of where Mary stood watching the men.

Gorst announced to Pickett, "Sir, we've captured a spy. Or anyway an intruder."

Sutherland and McCleary escorted Ike Webster up onto the porch.

Pickett said, "Good work, men. You can release him and get back to your posts."

As the soldiers dispersed into the fog, Pickett said, "Mister Webster, I believe."

Cutler said, "Ike. Fancy meeting you here."

Griffin exclaimed, "Why, dash it, man, you're completely winded! Come in, come in."

As Pickett and Cutler moved back into the hallway, Griffin escorted Webster, saying, "What the deuce have you been doing?"

Webster, still gasping for breath, said, "Rowed over… from Fort Townsend…Colonel Casey…General Scott…"

Pickett asked, "What about Colonel Casey? I haven't asked for reinforcements."

Webster said, "Well, somebody must have. He's out tryin' to scrounge up a boat to bring 'em here."

Griffin said, "Won't do him much good for a few days yet. Can't get through the pass." Explaining to Mary: "Currents are too dicey through there on these tides." To the other men: "Might be able to land 'em on the west side or up at the north end if the fog lifts in the morning."

"And what about General Scott?" Pickett asked.

"On his way," said Webster. "Left the Columbia River yesterday. Could be here any time."

Webster paused for breath, then said, "Looks like we're finally gonna have a shootin' war."

Mary said, "Well, it's about time they made up their minds!"

All the men looked at her in surprise.

"Oh, I didn't mean…of course I don't want a war. It's just that all this waiting and wondering is keeping…certain people… too busy for…well, it's all very unpleasant."

Pickett said, "I must admit that the waiting has been difficult for some of my men."

Marlene sniffed unsympathetically, stepped forward and said, "And what do you suppose it's like for the men in the ships, all cramped up with a thousand others while a few Yankees have this whole island to move around on? And all the while that nice Mister Campbell running all over the place trying to settle the whole thing peacefully. I've no patience with the lot of them."

Marlene paused for breath, then added, "If you'll pardon me saying so."

Cutler said, "That's it! That's how we can stop this thing! Marlene, I could kiss you!"

Marlene glanced frigidly at Mary, then looked directly at Cutler.

"I'm sure you could kiss anybody. Sir."

"Marlene," pleaded Cutler.

Marlene drew herself up into a haughty pose worthy of Queen Victoria herself.

"Okay. *Miss Potts*. But if you'd only let me explain… well, that'll have to wait. Ike, where'd you leave the boat?"

"That little beach you showed me over on the west side."

"Don't mind if I borrow it, do you?"

"No. But where are you going?"

"Fort Townsend. If I can reach either Casey or Scott in time, we might be able to stop this thing."

Griffin said, "You mean to cover twenty miles of open water in fog so thick you could hardly cut it with a hatchet?"

"In a rowboat?" Pickett asked.

"Yep."

Webster said, "With a minus tide coming a little after midnight. The outgoing current'll probably pull you right out to sea."

Cutler said, "Well, I'll just have to chance it. If I don't see you all again, it's been nice knowing you."

Marlene shoved the dessert tray at Mary and ran up the hallway shrieking, "Lyman! Wait!"

Cutler paused and turned, and she hurled herself at him.

Pickett said, "I must point out to you, Mister Cutler, that this is a military matter."

Embracing Marlene, Cutler said, "I don't see how it

could be. Oh, you mean Colonel Casey and General Scott and the war. Well, I guess I'm just an interferin' sort of a fella."

Cutler kissed Marlene. She responded, and they gave it their undivided attention for longer than was, strictly speaking, proper in the presence of others.

Griffin, impressed, said, "By gad, my boy!"

Cutler released Marlene, told Pickett, "Don't start any shooting while I'm gone" and hurried away into the fog.

Webster shouted after him, "There's a compass in the boat!"

To himself he added softly, "For whatever the hell good that'll do him."

~26~

Fort Townsend lay under patchy late-night fog as a sidewheel steamer dropped anchor in the bay. Deckhands lowered a boat. Oarsmen climbed down to the boat, followed by an officer. The boat was cast off, and the oarsmen pulled for the fort's pier.

General Harney was about to prepare for bed when a knock came at the door of his quarters.

"Who is it?" he bellowed.

"Corporal O'Brian!" replied a voice from outside the door.

"Come in!" Harney commanded, and Corporal O'Brian came in.

Coming quickly to attention, the corporal announced, "Lieutenant Galloway to see you, General."

"Who the hell is Lieutenant Galloway?"

"Adjutant to General Scott, sir."

"What's he doing here. What does he want?"

"To see you, sir. Immediately, he said."

Harney growled, "Damn! Well, tell him I'll be with him in a minute."

The corporal turned and left.

Almost exactly a minute later, Harney walked out into the front room of his quarters where Lieutenant Galloway stood respectfully waiting for him.

Galloway said, "My apologies, General, for this late call."

"What's the reason for it?"

"General Scott presents his compliments and instructs me to escort you to his ship."

"Scott's ship? You mean he's here?"

"Yes, sir."

"What does he want?"

"I hesitate to say, sir."

"Don't be coy with me, Lieutenant! What does the old boy want?"

"With all due respect, then, General Scott wishes to know what the hell you think you're doing. And he expects you aboard his vessel in fifteen mnutes to satisfy him on that point."

The rhythmic clatter of a big steam engine gave advance notice, if anyone had been nearby to hear it, of the *Sylvia*'s cautious progress through the dense fog off the southwest end of San Juan Island. On the enclosed lower deck, the Purser stood guard over all the paraphernalia of a small military force on the move, which included the rifles of the soldiers who clogged the open upper deck as they peered vainly into the fog.

In the wheelhouse, Colonel Casey and the *Sylvia*'s Captain stood on either side of the helmsman.

Casey said, "I'd much prefer to land around on the east side. If the British see us going ashore, they may think twice before making their move."

The Captain replied, "We couldn't even find the pass in this fog. And if we did, we couldn't get through it on this tide. We could go around the north end and down the other side. We might get there by sun-up."

"I'd like to get my men into position sooner if possible," said Casey. "Let's turn around and try to run in just a little closer this time. There must be some place on this side where we can get ashore."

General Scott and General Harney stood on the deck of the sidewheel steamer still anchored in the bay off Fort Townsend.

"It is clearly understood, then" said Scott, "that from this moment I am in command."

"Understood, General," Harney replied.

Scott watched Harney climb into the boat that waited to carry him back to the shore, which was visible as isolated areas of darkness in the patchy fog.

The small steam-powered double-ender that had carried Campbell and the newspaper reporter through the San Juan Islands now glided slowly through the fog. The skipper's young boy was asleep under a tarp stretched across the forward end of the boat. Cutler manned the pump while the skipper steered the boat and scanned the thin fog along the starboard side for occasional glimpses of land. Cutler's rowboat sloshed along in their wake, secured to the double-ender by the rope that had earlier secured it to a driftwood log.

"That oughta be Point Wilson," said the skipper, pointing to a low headland rising out of the water-level fog. "Keep an eye on the shore. I've gotta stay far enough out to miss the rocks."

The boat slid out of the fog into a world that was darker in spite of the visible stars and the unseen moon, then back into the weirdly lighter world of the fog. Eventually sounds of shipboard activity came from somewhere ahead. The skipper steered in the direction the sounds appeared to come from, and soon the upper portions of a large side-wheel steamship appeared in the thinner fog ten feet above the water. At that moment, a voice called out, "Ahoy there! Steer clear!"

Cutler abandoned the pump and shouted back, "I'm looking for General Scott! Do you know where I can find him?"

The unseen voice replied, "State your business!"

By this time, the hull of the steamship was visible. Cutler shouted, "I've just come from San Juan Island! I need to talk to General Scott!"

Another voice from aboard the ship commanded, "Bring that man aboard!"

Lieutenant Galloway stood on deck as Cutler climbed up the side of the ship on a sturdy wooden ladder. Deckhands were making ready to weigh anchor, which required Cutler to step lively and move aside frequently as he followed the Lieutenant to the shipboard equivalent of a drawing room.

General Scott stood in the center of the room as they entered. Lieutenant Galloway said, "General Scott, this man's name is Cutler. He says he's just come from San Juan Island."

"We're preparing to sail for San Juan Island immediately," Scott told Cutler. "How's the fog between here and there?"

"Bad," Cutler replied.

"How did you get here?"

Galloway said, "He arrived in a small steam launch."

"Better than what I started in," said Cutler. At the questioning looks on the others' faces, he went on: "I started out in a rowboat. Best I could do against the current was to keep it from pullin' me backwards. Wasn't able to make much progress down this direction. Lucky for me I got picked up by that fella with the steam launch."

"And just what did you want to talk to me about?" inquired Scott.

"I think I know how to stop this war before the shooting starts."

The ship's Captain entered at this moment and said, "We're ready to get underway, General."

"Go ahead," Scott said. "Mister Cutler, I presume you're at liberty to come with us."

"You bet."

"Good. Now, what is this plan of yours?"

At Camp Pickett, Cutler's sixty-six men crouched along the earthwork they'd constructed, straining to see the warshps in the bay through fog so dense that they couldn't even see the beach below them.

Along the high ground above the path leading down to the water, American settlers were deployed. Their widely spaced line ran from a corner of the fence surrounding the farmhouse to thick timber at the base of a hill several hundred yards away. They stood, knelt, squatted, or lay on the ground facing the bay with a tangled line of bushes behind them.

Jeremiah muttered, "Captain Pickett seems mighty pleased that we hold the high ground. But them Englishmen have got the whole rest of the island to come ashore on."

Zeke said, "But they're anchored right out there in

front of us. If they want to come ashore somewhere else, they've got to pull up their anchors and sail around to some other spot."

Cyrus Wilson said, "So what's to stop 'em?"

Zeke explained: "If they start pullin' up their anchors, we hot-foot it across the island and wait for 'em wherever they decide to land."

"I hate to ruin your battle plan," Tubby said, "but this island's something like twenty miles long and damn near as wide in places. If they pull up anchor, how're we gonna know where to go?"

Higgins put in, "And even if we could post lookouts at all the possible landing places, they'd never get word to the rest of us in time."

Zeke said, "Remember what Captain Pickett told us: it's a point of military honor for 'em to land right in front of our guns."

Jeremiah muttered, "From the looks of the guns on those ships, our guns won't matter much. They fire one round and there won't be enough of us left to care where they come ashore."

Higgins said, "I really wish Captain Pickett hadn't said we'd make a Bunker Hill of it if necessary."

"Bunker Hill was one of the most famous battles in our history," Zeke pointed out.

"Which we lost," Cyrus reminded him.

Lieutenant Galloway and the ship's Bosun stood at the bow of the sidewheeler doing what everyone else who happened to be outdoors in or near the San Juan Islands was doing that night: peering into the fog.

Galloway looked aft, then to the side, then forward again and said, "I thought another vessel was coming with us."

"Yes, sir," replied the Bosun. "The revenue cutter *Jefferson Davis*."

"I haven't seen or heard another ship since we left Port Townsend."

"You wouldn't hear much of her, sir, unless she was real close. She's under sail. And you wouldn't see her on a night like this. But she picked us up as we came out past Point Wilson, and she's back there somewhere."

"There isn't much wind. Can she keep up with us?"

"She's a tops'l schooner, so she'll catch whatever breeze there is. And there's enough to move her," said the Bosun.

Suddenly the steamship lurched violently and the deck tilted, sending the Bosun sprawling over the capstan and Galloway to his knees against the rail.

"Damn!" shouted the Bosun. "Beggin' your pardon, sir. We're aground."

"In the middle of the Strait of Juan de Fuca? I thought the only thing out here was Smith Island."

"I'm pretty sure this *is* Smith Island, sir."

A puff of breeze dissipated enough of the fog to reveal

a beacon light on a short wooden tower fifty yards away.

"And that'd be the Smith Island light, sir," said the Bosun.

With a *crunch* and a tremendous *crack*, the ship lurched again, sending both men staggering a few steps aft.

"Son of a bitch!" yelled a voice in the fog beyond their stern.

The Bosun said, "And that'd be the *Jeff Davis*."

In the fog along the high ground above San Juan Town, McGregor crept out of the trees on the flank of the settlers' line of defense. He carried two jugs of moonshine. Handing one to the nearest settler, he said, "Here's a little something to keep you warm. Don't hog it."

The settler pulled the cork, took a gulp, choked and coughed, then took two smaller swallows before recorking the jug and taking it to the next man along the line.

McGregor picked his way among rocks and small trees to the other end of the line and handed the other jug to Zeke, saying, "Same stuff we're selling at the store. Hope you like it."

"Thanks," Zeke said. Then he pulled the cork, sipped, smacked his lips, took two longer sips, corked the jug and passed it on to Clarence.

Scott, Galloway, and the sidewheeler's Captain stood

on the aft deck looking at the splintered bowsprit and smashed rail of the *Jefferson Davis* which were intimately entwined with the remains of their own vessel's taffrail. The Captain of the *Davis*, standing on his foredeck, asked, "Are you badly damaged?"

"No," answered the steamer's Captain, "but we're stuck. The next tide high enough to float us won't be until tomorrow night!"

"How about you?" called Scott. "Are you seaworthy?"

"Yes."

"And afloat?"

"Yes. We're lowering the boats now to pull us free of your vessel."

"Can you take a few of us aboard?"

"By all means."

To Galloway, Scott said, "Get Mister Cutler. We're going to San Juan Island come hell or high water."

Galloway smiled as he said, "Yes, sir."

Scott, also smiling but more grimly, said, "And since we're not waiting for high water, I hope we don't run into too much hell."

Shortly before dawn, Captain Hornby climbed aboard the *Beaver* from the gig that had carried him from his own ship, which was anchored nearby. He made his way to the Captain's cabin, where Sir James and Fainworthy awaited him.

Sir James said, "Why have you not yet landed your troops, Captain Hornby?"

"As I explained at our last meeting, Sir James…"

"You were reluctant to do anything to interfere with the boundary negotiations. Let me relieve your mind on that point. The negotiations have been suspended until this situation is resolved. So now you may attack at any time."

Hornby said, "But Admiral Baynes is due back…"

"We will not wait for Admiral Baynes. For the last time, Captain, I order you to occupy this island and remove every last Yankee from it."

"Very good, Sir James. As soon as the fog lifts."

Fainworthy sniffed.

"Yes, Mister Fainworthy?" said Sir James.

Fainworthy said, "I beg your pardon, Sir James. But one would have thought that the fog would provide excellent cover. The element of surprise, as it were."

Hornby said, "The Americans know we're here. No doubt they're watching us at this moment…or would be if they could see through this fog. But even if they couldn't see us, I'm sure the sounds of a thousand marines climbing into boats with their weapons and being rowed ashore would attract their attention."

Fainworthy said, "If the element of surprise is of no military value, how about your cannons? Bang away into the fog for a few minutes and you will destroy their camp and most of them with it."

"Along with Bellevue Farm," said Hornby. "And its inhabitants. It's difficult to aim a cannon precisely, especially at a target you can't see."

"I hadn't thought of that," said Fainworthy.

"I had," said Hornby.

Sir James said, "Very well, Captain. I leave the conduct of the affair to you. But I want this clearly understood: the moment the fog lifts, you attack."

"Yes, Sir James," said Hornby.

At Camp Pickett, the soldiers at the earthwork took turns napping. Sutherland said, "I'd rather be back up at Whatcom growin' turnips than sittin' here waitin' for this fog to lift."

Gorst said, "When it does lift, you'll *really* wish you were growing turnips again."

Along the civilian defense line, nerves were fraying.

Clarence said, "I feel like a sitting duck."

"Me, too," said Tubby. "I'd feel a whole lot safer if this fog would lift."

Jeremiah said, "They could be coming ashore this very minute and we'd never know it."

Higgins responded in a loud whisper: "You might if you'd shut up and listen!"

They all hunched forward, cocking their heads to catch any sound that might come to them out of the fog.

Light fog, gentle breezes, and patches of blue sky accompanied the sunrise over the Victoria waterfront. The British flagship *HMS Ganges* was arriving at the wharf. Teams of sailors hauled on mooring lines which had been looped around bollards on the wharf, pulling the ship closer. As the sailors secured the mooring lines, a crowd of civilians on shore watched other sailors run out the gangplank.

Admiral Baynes crossed the gangplank and looked around in surprise at the level of activity so early in the morning. Sailors, merchants, loungers, drifters, and sightseers were out and about.

A newsboy near the wharf called, "Latest news from the theater of war!"

Baynes summoned the newsboy and asked, "War? What war?"

"The Pig War, sir," said the newsboy.

Baynes, startled, asked, "What Pig War? Where?"

"San Juan Island, sir. Captain Hornby's there wtih five ships and a thousand marines."

"Dear God! How many casualties?"

"None yet, sir, except the pig."

"This is preposterous!" Baynes muttered as he hurried back aboard the *Ganges*.

To the First Mate, Baynes ordered, "Cancel all shore leave. All hands to their stations. Prepare to cast off and make sail."

The newsboy worked his way along the street shouting, "Admiral Baynes goes to the scene of battle! Read our next edition in one hour for all the latest news!"

The fog on Haro Strait between Vancouver Island and San Juan Island was dissipating. The overhead veil had already thinned enough to show patches of blue sky, and even on the water there were large fog-free zones.

General Scott and the Captain of the *Jefferson Davis* stood at the starboard rail catching an occasional glimpse of rocks, trees, or open ground along the shoreline.

"We're heading northwest," explained the Captain. "We can't take the channel between San Juan and Lopez, so we'll have to go up around the north end."

"How long will that take?" Scott asked.

"Hard to tell," replied the Captain. "It depends on…"

"Ship ho!" called the lookout from somewhere above

them. "Port side!"

"Fall off!" called another voice from elsewhere on the *Davis*. "Ten degrees starboard!"

At that moment the *Ganges* appeared out of the fog fifty yards off their port side on a course almost parallel to that of the *Davis*. A voice came from the *Ganges:* "Port the helm! Twenty degrees!"

Scott and the Captain hurried to the port side as the ships gradually reduced their angle of convergence and advanced side by side.

"Ahoy!" called the lookout on the *Ganges*. "What vessel are you?"

The lookout on the *Davis* called back, "United States revenue cutter *Jefferson Davis*! What vessel are you?"

"Her Brittanic Majesty's ship of war *Ganges*!" shouted his counterpart across the water.

Scott shouted across the water, "Let me speak to the highest-ranking officer aboard your ship!"

An officer appeared at the rail of the *Ganges* and asked, "Who wishes to speak with Admiral Baynes?"

"I do!" shouted Scott. "General Scott. Commanding General of the United States Army!"

Baynes appeared at the rail beside the other officer as the ships moved closer to each other on exactly parallel headings.

"I am Admiral Baynes!"

Scott said, "I wish to make a proposal for ending this

war without bloodshed!"

Baynes replied, "I am on my way to San Juan Island with the same end in view. Will you come aboard and join me? We can discuss the matter en route."

Scott looked down at the motion of the two hulls rolling gently twenty yards apart and said, "Thank you, Admiral. But I'm a little bruised from the night's events, and I'm not as young as I used to be."

"My apologies, General. May I come aboard your vessel?"

"By all means!"

At commands from their officers, sailors on both ships prepared to drop sails and throw lines to pull the ships together.

Over Bellevue Farm and San Juan Town, the fog was beginning to burn off.

On the high ground, the settlers began to grow uneasy at the fulfillment of their overnight wish.

"We're mighty exposed up here," observed Cyrus.

"Maybe we oughta move back a little," Clarence suggested. "Just until they start coming ashore."

Word spread along the straggly line of civilians, and one by one they crept back into the bushes and small trees. Some of them emerged, backwards, into the open grassland behind the bushes and stood up to peer over them.

When Pickett, watching the ever-more-visible activity aboard the British ships, saw Hornby climb into a gig, he turned and headed for the path down to the water. By the time Hornby's gig reached the beach, Pickett was there to greet him.

At Camp Pickett, the watching soldiers saw the *Jefferson Davis* appear from around the wooded headland near the pier.

"That's one of our ships!" said McCleary. "Looks like somebody finally decided to send us some reinforcements."

"Look!" put in Gorst. "She's been hit! She's took damage!"

Sutherland said, "So there's been action somewhere. Looks like this war's finally started."

On the beach, Pickett and Hornby exchanged the obligatory bows.

Pickett asked, "How may I have the honor of serving you, Captain Hornby?"

Hornby said, "I have the honor to inform you, sir, that my orders are to open fire with my ships' guns immediately and to land my troops…a few minutes later."

"And I remain under orders to oppose your landing."

"Forgive my impertinence, Captain Pickett…is it your intention to carry out those orders to the fullest extent?"

"It is."

Hornby sighed, then said, "You have my deepest admiration, sir. And my very deepest regret."

On the high ground, the settlers had a clear view of the gun crews preparing to fire their cannons. Zeke stepped behind a tree trunk, tripped over a root, and fell against a tangle of vines and branches which collapsed under him: it was a camouflage screen, and behind it McGregor lay sleeping beside his hidden still.

Half awake now, McGregor sat up and said, "What… who's that? What's going on?"

Zeke, thrashing around in a vain effort to extricate himself from the vines and branches, staggered closer to the still.

McGregor struggled to his feet saying, "Careful! Start a fire if ye're not careful!"

Zeke fell against the still, and the fire under the boiler immediately ignited the dry leaves in the vines that still clung to his legs.

As he shook himself free of the burning leaves, they scattered into grass that had been left so dry by the summer weather that it ignited instantly in spite of surface moisture left by the night's fog.

"Did start a fire," mumbled McGregor.

Gentle air movement carried the flames to the dry bracken among the trees and bushes.

At Camp Pickett, the soldiers were at their posts along the earthwork, their rifles aimed at the beach.

Aboard the ships, the gun crews stood by their loaded cannons.

As smoke began to rise from the high ground above the path, McGregor lurched out of the bushes, threw back his head, and yelled, "Fi…"

Instantly Zeke's hand was clamped over McGregor's mouth. Clarence, Tubby, and Higgins ran to help subdue McGregor before he could free himself from Zeke's grip. On their third attempt, they succeeded in persuading McGregor that the word he had been about to utter would have had seriously adverse results.

On the beach, Hornby and Pickett looked up at the smoke.

"That grass is as dry as tinder," Pickett said.

Hornby said, "May I offer asistance, Captain?"

"Thank you, Captain," Pickett replied.

On the high ground, settlers stamped on the flames.

Farmhands came running with rakes which they used to pull burning grass away from the scorched areas and roll it back, snuffing out the flames. Others raked burning bracken out of the bushes using the same technique. Still others brought shovels and began throwing dirt on the rapidly expanding ring of flame.

The oarsmen from Hornby's gig arrived carrying their water-soaked tunics, which they began using to beat out the flames.

Soldiers from Camp Pickett came with buckets of water which they sloshed along the perimeter of the fire and into the bushes where spot fires were breaking out.

In a few minutes the fire, in all its locations, had been extinguished. Settlers, soldiers, farmhands, and oarsmen shook hands all around.

As the oarsmen returned to the beach, Pickett said, "Thank you, men." To Hornby he said, "And now I presume we'll be getting on with our war."

Hornby, seeing Baynes, Scott, and Cutler being rowed ashore from the *Jefferson Davis*, said, "Perhaps not."

~ 30 ~

In the Bellevue Farm dining room, Admiral Baynes, Captain Hornby, General Scott, Captain Pickett, and Lyman Cutler sat around the table.

Baynes said, "Joint military occupation. How perfectly obvious."

"A token force representing each side," said Scott, "with arms and ammunition appropriate to their number and the peaceful intention of their mission."

Baynes added, "And the boundary issue to be submitted to an international court of arbitration for settlement."

Hornby said, "Speaking for all of us, Mister Cutler, thank you for your excellent suggestion."

Scott asked Baynes, "Do you think Governor Douglas will approve the plan?"

"I have the authority to approve it," replied Baynes. "And I do."

The clean-up of San Juan Town which Higgins and the other settlers had long hoped for was finally underway.

Sutherland, McCleary, Gorst, Alf, Tom, Will, and Jack supervised as drifters, gamblers, hooch merchants, and ladies of ill repute took down tents and dismantled shanties, carrying most of their materials and possessions to boats pulled up on the beach. Some boats were already leaving the bay.

In the hardware and dry goods store, the saloon had been converted back into a retail establishment. Bottles and jugs remained on the shelves behind the counter. Hanging from the beer keg was a placard reading *Bar Open Saturday Nights Only*.

Ike Webster, Sam Pike, and Higgins were admiring the restoration when Griffin came through the door.

"Finally got rid of all the hooch merchants, eh?" said Griffin. "Capital, capital."

"Not quite all of 'em," Webster said. "I've had the American authorities make out one license to sell liquor on this island."

Higgins proceeded to hang a framed document on the wall between the shelves and the door leading to the back premises.

Pike said, "And I've issued one license from the English authorities."

Higgins hung a second framed document on the wall. Griffin said, "By Jove, that ought to keep things under control."

On the path in front of Bellevue Farm, a British surveyor and an American surveyor stood examining maps.

The American surveyor, pointing up the path to the hilltop beyond Cutler's cabin, said, "I think I'll recommend a camp on the open ground up there. Good visibility but convenient to this harbor."

The British surveyor said, "I think I'll recommend a camp on one of these harbors up on the northwest corner. Right across the strait from Victoria."

"And what about a road connecting the two camps?" suggested the American.

"Excellent idea. Why don't we borrow a couple of horses from the farm and ride out to look over the terrain?"

The surveyors passed through the gate and went around the farmhouse toward the barn as Cutler came down the path. At the same time, Fainworthy came up the path and tried to ignore Cutler as they reached the gate together.

"Howdy, Fainworthy," said Cutler. "Say, too bad you never got a chance to serve that warrant. But I guess you can put it up on your wall as a memento of the Pig War."

Fainworthy replied, "Permit me to say that your rustic sarcasm is not appreciated."

"Okay," Cutler said with a smile, "I permit you to say it."

"And one more thing, Mister Cutler. I...that is to say, Sir James...may have failed to prevent you from interfering in matters that are none of your concern, but I must insist that you stop inflicting your attentions on Miss Griffin."

Marlene came out of the farmhouse, saw Cutler, and rushed out through the gate and into his arms.

Fainworthy blurted, "You, sir, are a cad and a bounder!"

Captain Hornby and Mary came out of the house, her hand delicately resting on his forearm. As they approached the gate, she said, "Hello, Mister Cutler. I hope you're feeling well after your busy night. Potts, you may have the rest of the afternoon to yourself. Mister Fainworthy, I believe you know Captain Hornby."

Hornby and Fainworthy nodded at each other.

As Hornby and Mary started down the path, she said, "It must be terribly exciting to play such an important role in the destiny of the empire, Captain Hornby."

"I wish you'd call me *Geoffrey*," he said. "And would it be presumptuous of me to call you *Mary*?"

As they continued down the path, Fainworthy stood watching them like a man recently struck by lightning and uncertain whether or not he's still alive.

"What you need, Fainworthy," Cutler said, "is a certain directness about you."

"What?" mumbled Fainworthy.

"A sort of zest," added Cutler.

Fainworthy recovered enough of his composure to

look at Cutler.

"I beg your pardon?"

Cutler added, "Oh, and lilac water."

Fainworthy assumed his most aloof demeanor and walked away down the path.

Cutler said to Marlene, "I'm afraid Fainworthy's right. I'm just an interferin' sort of a fella. Now, I kinda hate to go interferin' in your plans, but I have another idea to propose."

Nearby, finches flitted from bush to bush and insects buzzed in the tall grass. In the trees, nuthatches hung in bizarre positions from the branches and trunks. Over the bay, gulls swooped and soared.

High above the island, a bald eagle circled slowly and possessively.